Confound

Teresa Lucas

TERESA LUCAS

ISBN-13: 978-0-9907663-08

ISBN: 0990766306

Printed in the United States of America

10 9 8 7 6 5 4 3 2 1

TERESA LUCAS

DEDICATIONS

To You

TERESA LUCAS

CONTENTS

ACKNOWLEDGMENTS

Thank you to those who believe in me and pushed me to believe in myself.

Thank you to my best friend Toya who have always had my back no matter what, my mother who supports me unconditionally and a special thanks to my cousin Crystal. This book is for people out there who have an imagination that others may not understand but can be used to openly express themselves and encourage others to do the same.

Thank You

TERESA LUCAS

Chapter One

Another day in the great city of Chicago. I been here
most of my life and love it despite the up and down
weather. Like any other day I woke up, made myself
breakfast, got dressed and headed out the door to start
my day. I called Arashi on my way out the door
because she always try to sleep through the day.

"Get up"

"It's too early for your shit Adena. Why do we always
have to get up this early?"

"Because you have nothing else to do and we have a
business to run"

"Sleep is something to do. Now leave me alone"

"Get your ass up. I'm on my way Arashi"

"ARASHI"

"I heard you the first time. You don't have to yell"

"See you in a few" I said before I ended the call.

I went to meet Arashi at our spot to train and make plans for later on tonight. We meet here every day to train because it's private and allows us to use our abilities without being noticed. Yes abilities. The thing is, Arashi and I have been linked to each other since childhood.

We never knew how or why but every day we try to find out the truth about who we are. Compared to normal people we blend in but there are things about us that stand out. I have long brown hair, bright hazel eyes and I am average height, which makes it easy for me to blend in.

My skin is very rich and caramel. Even more important, our eyes. My eyes turn true red and Arashi's ice blue. This is what happens when we're mad. Arashi is fierce. She's tall with long pure black hair, light skin and light hazel eyes. Her features are perfection. But she is deadly in every way.

Our meeting place is near Arashi's place which is located in Willow brook, IL in the middle of what looks like a forest. Lots of trees and nobody ever walking through it so we can always use our abilities without being seen.

It took me about thirty minutes to make it to our spot. Arashi is always late so I start my training with a few warm ups and stretching.

Today was supposed to be a regular day but when I got to our spot I already sensed the change in the atmosphere. The intensity and pull in the air was my que to be prepared. When I walked through the trees and made it to where we usually meet I was greeted by a young man with an undying beauty.

He is average height with light skin. He couldn't be no more than 17, very beautiful and elegantly dressed. But what really caught my attention were his eyes. The same as me and Arashi's light hazel brown.

"May I help you?"

"I'm looking for Adena."

"Who are you?"

"My name is Dante and I'm looking for Adena. Are you her?"

His voice was angelic like, deep and rich enough to draw another person into a daze just by listening. He had a pull not like Arashi and I share but one that feels oddly familiar.

"I am Adena as you know already or you wouldn't be here. What is it you want?"

He smiled at me and I couldn't get pass how beautiful he is. Beauty is something we both have but he stands out more. Almost breathtaking.

"What I want isn't important. Where is Arashi?"

"Why will I tell you that?"

"Considering it will be easier but I can find out the hard way."

That made me smile. He clearly had no idea what he was getting his self into. So I smiled and said

"Please do."

His smile disappeared and his voice was cold when he said to me

"As you wish."

He attacked with precise movement, balance, speed and strength as we do. He moved like a perfect dance partner. He attacked, I countered. He was good but his abilities were weak compared to mine. I treated him as a new student in my dojo learning the basics. This made him mad as I can tell now that he was putting all his strength in his attack and getting tired from hitting nothing but air. I could do this all day but my goal is to find out what he want. With a vicious attack of strength I hit him mid chest sending him flying across the forest. I was pinning him against a tree before he had a chance to blink but I didn't need to use force. My regular strength was enough to keep him from moving. So I held him against the tree with one hand over his heart just in case I wanted to crush it.

The look in his eyes was surprising. He really came here not knowing his target.

"You are looking for us yet you know nothing of us or this situation wouldn't be a surprise to you. Where did you come from and why are you looking for us?"

"We were sent here for one reason and that reason is to hunt you down and kill you."

That enraged me so I put more force into my hold pushing his chest in, making him cry out from the pressure on his heart.

"Why?" I snapped. "Who will be stupid enough to try and kill us?"

He started to laugh as if we were having a pleasant conversation and what I said was nothing but a joke. I pushed in more on his chest with the intent to kill until he screamed out in pain.

"Stop, you cannot save yourself if you kill your only source of information."

"Information is not a necessity for me. I know who you are from your training. It would have been in your best interest to just come out and tell me but since riddles are your attempt to get my attention killing you will just prove how right I am when your father sends more people."

"It doesn't matter what you think you know. Your main concern should be for who's coming for you."

"None of you have the strength or ability to kill us. The fact that you're trying is a joke."

"We might not be able to kill you, but we can distract you."

He looked at me with a slight smile on his face as realization hit me just what he was doing. He was trying to keep me occupied. The smile left his face when my reaction didn't go as he planned. Before he can take another breath I spent him around and crushed his spine leaving him paralyzed. The pain was unbearable for him but satisfying to me as I ran full speed out the forest to go to Arashi's place. She didn't stay far and I didn't want her to come unaware of what's going on.

"Arashi" I called out when I made it to her house. Arashi is confident in her own and takes no crap from no one. Not even me. She's very out spoken. I like this about her. Arashi is more than willing to use force. Trust me you don't want to go there.

"I don't know why you get there so early, you know I will be late. What's up?"

"Do you remember a boy named Dante?" I asked to see if she remembered the little boy who use to train with us before he was taken by his father.

"I don't." Arashi responded.

"I had a run in with him just now and he fights with precise movement, balance, speed and some strength as we do."

"Really?" Arashi said surprised.

"We need to find out what's going on."

7

We thought about it for a minute. Going over it in our heads. Every and anything that lead to us has been erased. His training can only come from one person and he's dead.

We need to find out what's going on, why is he here now? What's going to happen?

"I left him paralyzed at our spot. You ready?"

"Always am let's go."

Dante wasn't in good shape but like us he should be able to heal himself soon. He looked at me with passion in his eyes. There was no pain, fear or concern. He seemed like he was right where he wanted to be.

"You seem to be comfortable in our presence." Arashi said.

"I am content with the situation. I do not fear dying." Dante responded

"That is good but death won't come your way just yet." I was going to get information out him one way or the other.

"I see. There's no need to torture any information out of me. I am here as a messenger anyway."

"Then please enlighten us. What is your message?"

He looked at me attempting to hold my gaze which means the message is attended for me. So I gave him a smile and sat down on a tree bark right in front of him.

"That's Arashi?"

"You tell me"

"She looks like you. Am I right? Or is this an attempt to throw me off. It won't help you get away."

It was an attempt to piss me off so I played the role.

"Either you tell me who sent you or I'll make sure you endure a greater torture beyond the gates of hell."

"They do not lie; you are indeed a force to be reckoned with."

"Then don't test my patience" I snapped.

"Indeed, I am not sure why you are being targeted, but I can help you find out if you will allow me to assist you."

"Why?" Arashi asked.

"All I know is that she is not like you. She is a great deal more powerful. Her abilities will outweigh anything anybody will ever see." Dante said looking at Arashi

"How do you even know we exist?" I asked.

"It was all in the scrolls written by sensei Arobi and the rest foreseen."

"Your father doesn't have the ability of foresight." I said.

"No but grandfather does" Dante replied.

Grandfather was our sensei who taught us the history and technique of Japanese jujitsu. He raised us as his own family and took care of us. With him we learned of other abilities that didn't start to play a part until we hit puberty. He noticed that we were not as others and began training us how to master our abilities and not let them control us. We owed him everything. When he died his son took over his dojo and closed it down. We didn't care considering we had already finished our training and it was time to move on and blend with the real world. All connections to us died along with sensei Arobi. His son had no knowledge of our abilities but his grandson often trained with us and witnessed it. He was a kid then like us. Younger though. When his father came and took him away he was too young to have remembered what had happened after all those years. Dante was that grandson which explains why he fights like us but not how he looks or share our strength.

"Even if grandfather foreseen this how would your father know? We were there until his death."

"Grandfather kept a scroll of all his foresights of you in hopes of finding another sensei to take his place and keep you all safe. He wrote it down so that the person who took his place can start where he left off in hopes of protecting you. The scrolls were to be kept safe and kept away from those who planned on doing harm with them which is why each sensei had to take an oath guarded with their life. My father got a hold of the scrolls and couldn't believe what he had just discovered. From that day forward he started training us for this day. But he, as did I, did not have an idea of your full strength. That was the one thing that was left out of the scrolls."

"This is why you were surprised when I attacked you with a full blow."

"Yes. My goal was to come here and test you to see how much of an edge you have on me. But when I fought you, you didn't even use your full strength on me. I knew warning you about the hit on your life would get you to give me a real fight but I wasn't expecting this."

"You came knowing we have abilities. It should not have been that alarming."

"I did, but growing up I always been stronger, faster and moved more smoothly than anyone else including my father. That is why he sent me. He figured we would be on the same level of some sort but I found out otherwise."

"Why is it that you look and move like us?" Arashi asked.

"That I did not know until today when I attacked Adena. "

"Why does your father want us dead?" I asked.

"I'm not sure. But he doesn't mind killing you if he can't capture you."

"Why are you so forth coming with information about your father's plan?" I asked.

He looked at me with this bright smile on his face, looking like a falling angel and warrior.

"I'm here because I want to continue my grandfather's work. I don't wish to see my father destroy it. I only want to do what's right."

"So you will take the risk of deceiving your father and helping us do what exactly?" Arashi asked.

"Bring peace and continue grandfathers teaching for other's like us."

"Can you get up? If you try anything I will kill you." I said.

Arashi turned around as I sensed trouble heading our way. So did Dante.

"Who is it?" I looked at Dante.

"I don't know them"

I looked at Dante and gave him a firm look.

"If this is a set up you will die by my hands and my hands alone." Arashi snapped.

"I can ensure you this is not my doing"

"Then get ready to fight"

"With pleasure"

Arashi looked at me and shifted her eyes to Dante. I gave her a firm nod and told her in a thought we will kill him if he's lying. I expanded my senses to see just how close our attackers were and as I did they came swinging through the trees. Arashi went straight into attack mode sending everyone who came near us flying across the forest.

"Now this is a real training." Arashi smiled back at me. I smiled. No one loves a good fight more than Arashi. She was light on her feet moving, twisting and teasing them with her laugh as she took them out one by one with power hits that crushed their bones with one blow. She was having fun while they were feeding her appetite continuing to come at her.

I went pass them at a speed that they didn't even notice I was gone. Making them dizzy with confusion and sending them flying through the forest to their death. One gentle hit to the chest stopped their heart and they fell instantly to their death. When I made it back to Arashi she was waiting already finished off her bunch of fun. They were sent here with the confidence that they would succeed but all they got was death in return.

Arashi and I are linked somehow. We can hear each other thoughts and feel each other's pain. When I thought to myself it's time to go. She was right beside me with a look of satisfaction from her obsession for action.

"It's time to go. Dante just follow us." I said.

He nodded and we all went into a full speed run so that whatever standbys were around, we won't be seen. We headed to a place we called the safe house.

We made it to the safe house. It was time to plan our next move. The fact that someone would even target us is crazy. I have no intention of talking or making peace. I stood looking out the window trying to collect my thoughts. I forgot how beautiful it was out here in the forest. The safe house was far out in the middle of the forest where no one can get to it.

The only way to find this location is to know the exact location. We built this place from the ground up to look similar to Sensei Arobi dojo. It's the one place that keeps us connected to him at all times.

Everything was new inside and out but we made it look like it's been here for generations. Arashi walked in the room with a flow like she was walking on water. There was no need to ask each other if we were okay.

Besides we are linked. The difference between us is when she's mad her eyes turn pure ice blue. Almost like we are truly fire and ice.

"It was fun kicking some ass today. Too bad they didn't send more." Arashi said.

"Always a good stress reliever" I responded

"So when are we going to talk to Dante about what his father has been up to all these years?" Arashi asked.

"I just want to make sure we cover all the basis before we ask him."

"You think he's telling the truth?" Arashi asked me.

"No. I thinks he's hiding something." I said.

We didn't speak to each other, just read each other's thoughts. I have a plan that doesn't involve Dante much but he cannot know this. I need him to think we're working together while I find out just what's up Dante's sleeve. He helped us so far but he's hiding something that he doesn't want us to know. One way or another I will get it out of him.

We headed back down stairs to see what Dante was doing.

"What's going on?" Dante asked.

"We need to find out why your father wants us." I responded.

"We don't even know if were being lead into a trap." Arashi snapped at Dante. "You really want us to believe you don't know what Rin wants with us?" Arashi continued.

"I don't." Dante snapped back.

"That's bullshit." Arashi snapped again.

Dante needed to believe that we actually trust him enough to lead us to his father but not enough to reveal the dojo's hidden trails. I looked at Dante and then to Arashi. This was disturbing. I couldn't believe what was going on. It can't be right. Dante must have another plan that he wants to keep to himself just in case something goes wrong.

"Dante we are trusting you're not full of shit?" Arashi started snapping again.

"No, you are betting that I value my grandfather scrolls more than I do my life."

"I have some old friends I want to squeeze some information out of that will be helpful in more ways than one." I said.

17

"So we will stay here?" Dante asked.

"No, you will. That way I will know where you are." Arashi said keeping her gaze on Dante.

Arashi and I headed out. We being linked together really have its advantages but this was not one of them times. I really need some me time and of course Arashi knew exactly what I was thinking. Sex was on my mind.

"So you gone ditch me and go get you some huh?"

"Arashi get out of my head and yes. With the morning we had today I need a good release."

"That tells me exactly who you are going to see." Arashi laughed.

"This is disturbing. So I know you have a play date in mind as well." I said smiling at Arashi. She can always find someone when she's in the mood.

"Yes and were going to play until we can't play no more"

"You're a mess"

"Don't start acting like you not a freak Adena. I already know you are. You couldn't fool me if we weren't connected."

"I'm not denying it."

"Freak."

"Yea, yea, yea whatever."

We made it to the city and I dropped Arashi off at one of her friend's house. We agreed to meet back up in the morning. I headed to Quentin house. Quentin is one of the important men in my life. If I have a soul mate I am positive that it would be Quentin.

I made it to Quentin place right off the lake. I loved the view from here right off lake shore drive. Looking out and seeing nothing but water. He stayed on the 3rd floor of his building which made the view perfect. Nothing in the way to block it.

I gave a soft knock at his door as I always do and waited for him to answer. He opened the door and looked at me with a smile on his face that was enduring. He took my hand and led me into his place as he does every time I come over.

I couldn't take my eyes off him. The masculine sway in his walk, the firm way he held my hand like he will never let it go and the definition of muscles that ripped through his body had me wanting to attach myself to him in every way possible. He took me to the living room and turned on the TV just in case I wanted to watch it but my eyes never left him.

He didn't know how much of a tease he was being to me just by walking back and forth. He asked me a question but I didn't hear it. The only thing I was thinking was how much I can put his mouth to use.

"I'm sorry, what did you say?"

"I asked if you are hungry. I just finished dinner and I can make you a plate if you like."

"Yes I would love that thank you."

"No need, anything for you." Quentin said making me blush.

He walked away and I watched the tightness of his buttocks as they moved with every step he made. I just wanted to grab it and squeeze the tightness of his ass. I started imagining my hands on his ass as he penetrated in and out of me over and over again. My imagination took control of me because the next thing I know Quentin is standing in front of me asking me if everything is ok. Apparently I was moaning like my day dream was remarkably real. I suddenly realized my

eyes were closed and I open them and looked at
Quentin with passion in my eyes and couldn't hold
back anymore.

"Quentin"

I said his name in longing need with a soft whisper. All
I wanted him to do was satisfy everything my body
yearned for.

"Kiss me"

He put the plates of food down he had just made for
us and preceded to do exactly what I asked. He kissed
me with so much passion and heat at a slow rhythm
like he was playing a remedy with our lips and tongue.
I grabbed his face in hopes of intensifying our kiss but
he took my hands and pent them over my head. He
then moved his lips down to my neck and sucked me
like I was his favorite child hood sucker while using
simple strokes to slowly undress me.

He teased me every step of the way by not touching
me where I yearned for him most, the in's and out of
my folds on my lower lips and my aching peaked
breast. My lower body wept for him both vulnerable
and welcoming.

He began feeding my hunger and giving me soft kisses down my stomach till he reached my inner thighs. Kissing the outer area of my creases making me moan in satisfaction. He kissed the folds of my uterus and my body started to jerk beneath him.

I lay there in shock, stunned at how he was bringing me to a greater high with every touch and kiss he teased me with. I gave a shy shriek as he dived deeper with his tongue into my wetness. He was building me up for the ultimate climax. With seductive licks and his teasing tongue going in and out of me showing me how much appreciation he has in pleasing me.

My body still jerked and shivered under him yearning for more. I moaned, lifting my hips and twisting harder against him.

"Oh!" I moaned as he rubbed his staff against my folds while he watched me shiver in response.

"Quentin" His name was a demand for more, a need for him to take me whole.

"You want me to give you more"

"Yes!"

He slid only the head of his dick inside me with gentle strokes, and I gasped pushing myself up taking more. He withdrew it, pushed the head back in again and again. I watched as it went in and came back out wet and smooth with my inner desires all over it.

The feeling was nice but I was ready for something bigger and firm. He watched as he took it in and out and I tightened around every fucking movement. I reached to pull him in me but he stood his ground teasing me even more.

He started to caress my swollen pearl as he took his head in and out of me sending more vibrations through me and uncontrollable cries.

There was no way to win this tantalizing battle so I begin to play my own game. I begin touching myself, stroking and pinching my breast. I closed my eyes to get the full effect of the feeling. I cupped and squeezed my breast imagining it was his hands caressing me.

I brushed over and pinched my nipples displaying them like a work of art. Adding to the pleasure he was slowly giving me I opened my eyes and watched him as his eyes grew wide in excitement. I returned the tease with fierce passion in my eyes and a smile of pleasure on my face.

I closed my eyes as I felt him throb inside of me watching me tease and seduce him while I moan and bit down on my lower lip. I pulled and pinched my swollen nipples pulling them out at the same time tightening my grip around him as he throbbed more and more inside me.

Like a warrior being teased past his limits he cupped and latched on to my fully flushed nipple. With his mouth warm and wet he sucked on my nipple like it was his last supper, grabbing and squeezing it as he claimed it to be his. He squeezed with even more firmness inflecting more pleasure.

I cried out from the intense pleasure and arched my body as if trying to fit it all in his mouth. His hand holding my breast tight while I enjoy the pleasure and the pain. I lifted my legs around him in an attempt to swallow him whole as he put his hand beneath my ass lifting me as he grind into me.

He went in me with the greatest angle, catching my pearl while it's swollen and sensitive. He continued to pull on my nipple with his teeth. One last graze against my pearl and I climaxed. It suddenly came over me like a strong earthquake shaking me with non-stopping ripples giving me the ultimate sensation.

As if the pleasure couldn't get any greater he went completely inside me while I was shaking uncontrollably, tighten his grip with his hands intertwined with mine, moving at an intensive steady grind I felt him throbbing more and more inside me then he released, beginning his climax at the end of mine prolonging the feeling making it endless in time, Truly unforgettable.

Chapter Two

I woke up this morning in Quentin arms relaxed and
comforted. I replayed our night over and over in my
head smiling in remembrance. I got up quietly to look
out the window into the lake.

The waves were soothing and calm, inviting and
tempting. I regret having to leave after such a night.
Quentin got up and came to wrap his arms around me
while I enjoyed the view.

There was nothing else in the world I wanted more at
this time but this moment with him. I turned and
looked into those beautiful caramel brown eyes. I saw
love and warmth impelling my heart. It's hard but I
have to go. I broke the connection and went to put on

my clothes. Quentin stopped me and kissed me in a plea for me not to go.

"Adena, stay for breakfast."

"I wish I could but I have to go." The disappointment on his face felt like a stake being pushed through my heart. I wanted nothing more but to say yes, I just had to go.

"Come back soon."

"Always for you." He smiled with so much satisfaction and confidence as I confirmed my coming back to him.

"I'll hold you to that Adena."

"I know you will Quentin." I kissed him goodbye and walked out the door.

I headed to Arashi house so that we can start our unpredictable day. Arashi stayed in Willow Brook, Illinois not far from where we train. It doesn't take long to get there but I took my time so that I can enjoy the view of the lake.

I pulled into Arashi driveway and parked in front of the door. Arashi has a beautiful six bedroom seven baths brick stone house. It has dramatic two story windows bringing elegance to the estate. I walked straight in because Arashi never locks her door. She figure if someone was dumb enough to break in then why shouldn't she benefit from the extra training. The inside of her house is even more exquisite then the outside. When you walk in the door the first thing that catches your eyes is the long stairway of this two story house, hardwood floors throughout, and every piece of furniture is just as exquisite and antique looking all through the house. I stood standing in the foyer and called out to Arashi.

"Arashi"

"Upstairs"

I walked up the stairs and headed to Arashi's master bedroom. She was in her closet finding something to wear.

"Hey"

"What's up? How did everything go last night?" Arashi asked.

"Everything was great." I couldn't say it without putting this huge smile on my face and I should have known better because Arashi catches everything.

"The way you smiling it must have been more than great."

"Yea, yea, yea. What about you how was your night?"

"I did exactly what I said I was gone do. Played all night. Mum mum mum."

"Ok you could have kept the visual to yourself."

"You could have to but I thought mine was more exciting."

"Now who's the freak?"

"So what are we doing today Adena?"

"We are going to pay a visit to an old friend and try to squeeze some information out of him."

"Sounds like fun to me. Let me get dressed for some fun."

"Alright. I'm going to use your shower and borrow something to wear. I need to get out of these cloths."

"That's cool."

I got out the shower and went in Arashi closet to find something to wear. I should have known something loose and simple was not going to happen. Everything as usual was black. I grabbed some fitted black jeans and found a regular black shirt among all the half shirts. The one good thing was that Arashi loved flats. I found a pair of black boots and headed down stairs. I went to the kitchen where Arashi was making coffee.

"You really need to update your wardrobe. I can't believe everything is black."

"That's what I love best."

"How can you breathe in these clothes? They all are fitted."

"I like to show off my figure. If you going to complain you can always put back on what you had on."

"Yea, yea, yea."

"You want some coffee?"

"Yuck, no thanks. How about we pay Bruce a visit."

"Arobi's old friend?"

"Yes. He is the only person Arobi contacted when he needed something at the dojo. I can't help but to wonder if Sensei Arobi told him something."

"That means we have a long trip ahead of us."

"No we don't. Bruce moved to Chicago shortly after Arobi died. That's why I chose to come here just in case we needed to question him about who we are."

Bruce was one of Sensei Arobi's friends who came to

visit once a month at the dojo. They must have been close seeing that every time he came, him and Arobi talked and laughed amongst themselves for hours at a time. He will always give me and Arashi flowers called Azalea japonica snow. These are the most beautiful pure white scented Japanese flowers. Bruce always said to us

"If your heart is as pure as snow than your path will lead you to the true azalea within you."

Sensei Arobi always raised us to protect ourselves while Bruce made us remember the kid in us all in one day. He would take us for strolls through the forest to admire nature and swimming by the waterfall claiming that water is the true element of purity.

He treated us like we were goddesses in view of our beauty. Bruce watched as we grew up into beautiful happy young ladies until something neither of us was expecting happened. Sensei Arobi got sick. We never knew what caused the sudden illness we just figured he was getting old. Bruce came out to the dojo and stayed to take care of Arobi in his time of need.

To keep Arashi and me from dwelling on the situation

Bruce took over our trainings and still took us for our walks and swim allowing Arobi to rest. We often asked Bruce was Sensei Arobi getting better. Every time he will tell us *"Arobi is not worried where his path will take him so you should not worry for him. Remember what he has taught you and finish the path given to you."*

Arashi and I continued our days waiting for Arobi to get better. He didn't. Sensei Arobi got even sicker and his last words to us were *"I have taught you everything I know; now it is time to begin your journey. Always remember to listen to your heart and maintain your bond for it is your strength. Your beauty can be a blessing or a curse depending on the path you choose. Don't be afraid of what's coming ahead of you, fight with purity in your heart and you will win.*

Sensei Arobi died the next day. The days following his death his son took over the dojo and closed it. Bruce pleaded with him to keep it open and he would watch over us. Rin looked at us with eyes black as night you can feel the evil inside him. He told Bruce *"they are as dead to me as father is. He treated them like they were his children and me as I was nothing. I do not care what happens to neither them nor this place."*

Bruce helped us gather our things and took us to his place in the city near Harajuku station. We had just made 21 and it was time for us to be on our own. I found information about Chicago, IL at Bruce place so when he asked where we wanted to go I chose Chicago. Now comes the time for us to meet once again.

We arrived in Chinatown to pay Bruce a visit. He works at Colors Flowers & Gifts by the Chinatown gate. It wasn't a surprise that he worked with flowers seeing that he loves nature. We parked on kitty corner from the Chinatown gate and walked to his floral shop. When we arrived we walked in and were greeted by a short chubby man with long grey hair. His back was turned to us as he attended to a plant he was watering. I didn't need to see his face to know it was him. His hair was a little longer but he still had that relaxed voice tone.

"May I help you?"

"Yes we are looking for the Azalea japonica snow." He started laughing surprised that someone will ask for that flower here in Chicago.

"That is a very rare flower. You could not have seen it here in this state before. How do you know of it?" He then turned around and looked at me and Arashi. In that moment he dropped the water pot he was holding, starring at us in astonishment.

"It was given to us as a child to remember the purity in our hearts."

"Adena and Arashi."

"Yes. How are you Bruce?"

"I am okay. It is very nice to see how much you both have grown. I knew that this day will be coming."

"You knew that we will be coming to see you?" Arashi said with surprise in her voice.

"Yes. Arobi told me that one day you will come seeking answers to questions."

"Really?" I said with more anger than patience.

Before he can answer my question two men walked in the shop. Their presence felt like death, eye's black as night with a smile on their face like they have just caught their prey. They were 6 ft. tall and muscular. One with long black hair and pale skin, the other had shoulder length blond hair also pale skin. They looked the way they felt, like death.

Arashi being the ass she always is, spoke first. "Is it Halloween already? Sorry no candy here."

The men with the long black hair turned and looked at Arashi with his head tilted to the side as if he was intrigued with her. Then he finally spoke.

"You are very beautiful too bad I have to kill you."

They fought like ancient warriors hard and strong. They were able to keep up with our speed although we still had them on strength. We were tick for tack neither of us getting a hit off each other. I glanced over at Arashi noticing she was in the same boat as I was and ended up taking a blow from my attacker.

I flipped back landing on my feet in a crouched positioned then instantly lodging myself at him sending him flying into the wall. He got up, head cocked, looking at me like he had underestimated us. He came at me this time moving at an even faster speed, putting one hand around my neck.

I gave a strong blow to his arm as I spent, grabbed his shoulder and gave my finishing blow to his heart. He dropped to his knees but the blow did not kill him. My eyes turned fury red and I ripped his heart out of his chest. As I turned to assist Arashi her eyes had already turned ice blue. She flipped on his shoulders twisting around his neck decapitating him. We turned to face Bruce as our eyes changed back to normal.

"Bruce are you okay?"

He just stared at us for a moment until he finally said Kasai ya kori (fire and ice).

"Bruce." Arashi and I said together.

"Yes I'm okay."

"We should go." I said.

We headed back to Arashi house instead of the safe house considering we still needed to know what Bruce knew about us and Sensei Arobi scrolls. Dante was also another issue. We still need to know what he's not telling us. We arrived to Arashi house. Since we have already been attacked twice we decided to check the place out first. Arashi went through the front with Bruce as I took the back. There was nothing. We sat down in the living room to talk and figure everything out.

"Bruce we need you to tell us about Sensei Arobi's

scrolls. Did he tell you anything about who we really are?"

"Before Arobi died he told me of you and the importance of his scrolls. He wished for me to watch over you. That is why I moved to Chicago."

"We moved here because of you. I saw information about Chicago at your place so I thought since you were coming here we should too."

"Yes. Arobi told me that your path will lead you in Chicago so I gathered information and prepared myself for the move."

"But I don't understand how Arobi knew. If it wasn't for me seeing your information I don't know where we would be."

"Maybe that was the point. There's something here that connects you with who you are. Arobi must have known and set the idea in my head knowing you will follow."

"He knows us well." Arashi said entering the room while eating on a steak.

"I'm sorry do you want something to eat?"

"Yes!" I said mad that she was eating a steak without

me.

"I was talking to Bruce. You can make your own plate Adena."

"How Rude. I'm a guest"

"If that's what you want to call it."

Bruce started laughing at us bickering at each other like old women. This was typical of me and Arashi. When it came to food we played no games. I went in the kitchen to make me a plate and saw there was a full cooked meal. I know Arashi didn't cook this.

"Who cooked this? I know you didn't." I asked knowing Arashi could not have cooked a meal like this on her own.

"I hired a chef. I really wanted some steak." Arashi said.

"A true fat ass." I responded shaking my head.

"I take it you two love food a lot." Bruce said as he walked in the kitchen. He watched us dance to our own tones as Arashi made his plate and I made my own.

"Yes. I guess the dancing is too much huh." I laughed.

"No it's good you appreciate a good meal. It's not

every day your able to get a steak." Bruce smiled.

"That's exactly how I feel." Arashi said as she starts twirling in happiness over food.

We sat down and ate our food in silence. As much as we needed to know what was going on we were even hungrier. We were so tied up in the situation at hand I think this is our first real meal. The steak and potatoes were so mouthwatering I wiped my plate clean. I looked over at Bruce and he was still eating his food. He took his time and ate his food with patience so I went for seconds.

I knew Arashi was gone say something. When she thought fat ass I looked at her and stuck my tongue out on the way to the kitchen. I made me a second plate but stayed in the kitchen to eat it. My phone rings so I pulled it out of my pocket to answer. It was Quentin.

"Hello"

"I just wanted to hear your voice to make sure you ok."

"I'm fine. What made you think otherwise?"

"I was just surprised that you didn't stay yesterday."

"I Know I'm sorry there's something me and Arashi need to take care of and I will spend more time with you I promise."

"Ok, I will be waiting as always."

"See you soon." I hung up the phone longing to see him. Hearing his voice made my heart beat faster in anticipation.

"You know if you need another quickie you can go get one. We good here." Arashi said with a teasing grin on her face.

"Arashi I'm very tempted to kick you in the ass."

"I'm just saying Adena." Arashi started laughing repeating over and over rocky loves Emily. So I took one of her apples out her fruit bowl and threw it at her hitting her in the butt.

"Got you" I said laughing and running back to the living room to join Bruce.

"I'll get you back Adena. When you least expect it."

"Yea, yea, yea." I said as I sat down to restart our conversation with Bruce.

"Bruce what did Sensei Arobi tell you about us?"

"Not much. Just that you are special." Bruce

responded.

"What does that mean?" Arashi asked. We had been with Sensei Arobi since we were babies. We have no knowledge of our parents or where our abilities come from.

"You were born with the gift of fire and ice and the strength of a god. This is all he told me. The rest is in the scrolls."

"Then you must know that Arobi's son Rin has the scrolls." I said seeing that he was there when Rin closed the dojo.

"No. Arobi hid the scrolls so that no one can find them. I am the only one who knows the location. He trusted me to keep the scrolls hidden until the time came for you to know the truth." Bruce had an alarming look on his face.

"I'm sorry but it is true. He knows of our ability's and is responsible for the attacks on us."

"How? He should not know of the scrolls. How did he find out?" Bruce said with an alarming look on his face.

"Dante, Rin son told us of them. He claims to be here

to help us get the scrolls from his father so that he can continue his grandfather's wishes."

"That cannot be. Even if they have the scrolls all it holds are recordings of your trainings with Sensei Arobi. The scroll that tells who you are is written in code. It is impossible to decode without Sensei Arobi."

"How is it that Dante looks like me and Adena?" Arashi asked.

"I did not know he did." Bruce looks as surprised as we did. Like something is not adding up. Dante knows something and is not telling us or he is pulling our strings to try to find out what we know.

"I think it's time for us to question Dante again?" I said now more than ever wanting to kill him if he is setting us up.

"Dante is still here?" Bruce asked trying to put the pieces together.

"Yes. We left him at the safe house with the impression that we were going to help him get the scrolls back from his father."

"Do you think he's still there?"

"Yes. He couldn't leave if he tried. That's why we took

him there. It's protected. We turned on the alarm before we left. We are the only way he can get out."

"We should leave now." Arashi said.

I nodded in agreement. We left to go back to the safe house to question Dante but I still had a gut feeling something wasn't right. Although Sensei Arobi wanted to keep us a secret, he would have still passed his knowledge on to who he felt was the next protector of the scrolls. He would not have died before he succeeded. Bruce knew of our trainings but not of our parents which could only mean that he can't figure out Arobi's code to read the scroll either.

"Bruce do you think you can figure out the code to read Arobi scroll?" I asked seeing he knows of it.

"No I do not."

"Then why would he tell you about it?"

"I'm only meant to guide the next protector in the right direction."

"So is it possible that Dante is the next Protector."

"I don't know. It could be possible depending on how much he knows and where his information came from."

"He said his father."

"Rin only knows of your trainings, not your true abilities or who you are. He could not have informed Dante much about you."

I drove in silence going over and over in my head everything that happened today. Trying to put the pieces together and somehow figure out what was missing from the puzzle. Arashi interrupted my thoughts when she reminded me of Dante words.

"Dante said growing up he always been stronger and faster than everyone else including his father. He looks like us and have some of Arobi's training. Do you know why that is?" Arashi asked Bruce.

"No I don't. It must be something about it in the scrolls. Sensei Arobi would not have missed that."

"Well then it's clear we have to get the scrolls." I said as I sped up on the expressway.

I was in a rush to get to the safe house more now than later. I was speeding through traffic cutting in and out of traffic. I knew the possibility of getting pulled over and getting a ticket but this is Chicago. The police never pull over the people they are supposed to. The further out we got the clearer the road got. We were almost to the woods when I saw a car speeding behind us. Typically this will be normal but we were on a road that leads to a dead end. No one should be coming this way. I slowed down to see if it was just someone who lost their way and got my answer when they rammed into the back of my car. I sped up just to get some space between us and they rammed us again.

"Arashi can you take care of him please?"

"With Pleasure." Arashi climbed out the back window and got on the roof of the car. She stood up slowly not to gain her balance but to allow our pursuer to get a good look at her. She waved at them as they speed up to hit us again. With an inviting smile on her face thinking *yes that's it. Come on.* Arashi leaped into the air landing on the front end of the car sending it flipping in the air, over us and landing upside down in front of us. I immediately hit the brakes stopping right in front of the car.

"Bruce stay in the car."

"No problem." Bruce said as he gripped tight to his seat belt.

"Nice job Arashi. Very dramatic."

"I do what I can."

We walked over to the car to see who our pursuers were as they were climbing out of the car. It was another group of two. One was average height with an athlete's body. Carmel brown skin, Short cut hair and grayish light brown eyes.

He was dressed in regular light blue jeans and an all-white Hollister t- shirt. He was gorgeous. If he wasn't trying to run us off the road I would have actually been very aroused. The other one was rough looking but close to being beautiful. The right side of his face had a scar cutting throughout it looking like it was forged in with some type of heated metal. The other side was untouched, no scars, no bumps, no nothing. Almost as if it was perfection. Neither guy seemed like the killing type.

As we walked toward them they backed up away from us. They didn't attempt to run but wasn't trying to fight us either. Arashi and I looked at each other in confusion. We stopped in place and starred at the two men.

"Who are you?" I asked instead of attacking. I could have easily closed the distance between us and took him out but I didn't feel like I needed to. Although they tried to run us off the road. They didn't seem like a threat.

"My name is Nathaniel and this is my brother Joel." I looked over at his brother with the scars on his face as he kept his eyes on Arashi.

"For you to be the ones who attacked us you shouldn't be the one's backing up."

"It was not our intent to hurt you."

I started walking towards Nathaniel laughing in a get real way. He notices me pacing towards him and begins walking back.

"What did you think running us off the road would do?"

"Please we only intended to get you to pull over. We knew bumping your car would not have harmed you."

I closed the distance in a blink of an eye. He didn't seem surprised when I suddenly appeared in front of him. I attacked using basic fighting training underestimating Nathaniel. He retaliated protecting himself giving me a soft blow to the stomach pushing me a few steps back. I attacked again this time fighting at full strength but not really trying to hit him. I wanted to test him and see what he can do. He just blocked every attacked, turning and twisting away. I stopped.

"If you not here to fight, then what do you want?"

"We want to join in your endeavor to find out who you are." I looked over to Arashi and she shrugged her shoulders.

"Why do you want to assist us? How do you even know about us?" Arashi asked.

"When Rin put a hit out on you he included information about your abilities and pictures of the way you look. We didn't know there was others out there like us so we decided to come find you."

"We wasn't aware there was others either until today." We stood there for another minute looking over each other as I talked to Arashi mentally.

"Looks like we have more company?"

"Yes. What do we do now? They clearly are like us."

"I know. When I was just fighting Nathaniel he is clearly

skilled and trained. He could have given me a run for my money."

"I see that. I can feel how strong he is but his brother Joel is not as strong."

"So far we have four pieces to the puzzle that we need to put together and see where it leads us. Let's take them back to the safe house."

Arashi nodded in agreement as we turned and walked over to the car to get Bruce and fill him in.

"We are on our way to the safe house. You can join us." I said as we start walking towards the forest. Nathaniel looked at Joel and gave him a nod to come on. They followed us into the forest following the path. Arashi and I usually don't take a path because it's faster cutting straight through the trees. We had to consider the more logical route for Bruce.

"Bruce are you good with hiking?"

"It's been a while since I adventured through nature but I believe I can keep up." He smiled and followed in behind me and Arashi.

"It would be faster if we just carried him." Arashi said. Patience's is not a virtue of hers.

"Yes but we have other guest as well Arashi."

"We can keep up." Nathaniel said.

"You sure." I said as I turned to face Nathaniel.

"Yes." He answered.

"Joel you don't talk much huh?" Arashi asked.

"Only when being addressed." He said. He had a very soft tone to his voice. Not what you would expect from a boy who has scars as he does.

"Are you ok with running?" Arashi asked Joel.

"Yes I can keep up."

"Ok. Bruce you ready." I smiled at him waiting for his response.

"As good as I'm gone get."

"We will make it exciting just for you Bruce." Arashi said.

Bruce took a deep breath in and out and closed his eyes preparing himself for whatever. Arashi and I grabbed Bruce and took off running through the trees laughing and dancing in excitement. This was the first time today we have been able to enjoy the day. Bruce didn't seem worried about us running into a tree, dropping him or getting lost. He was enjoying nature, the feel of the wind hitting him as we ran, the smell of trees and water. We were all relaxed and enjoying the time to be at peace.

Nathaniel and Joel kept up with us as they said they would. They were more concentrated on where we were and where we were going. I could have told them they will never figure it out but I understood the feeling to know your surroundings at all times. As I paid more attention to the two of them, I saw that Joel looked up to Nathaniel and respected him. They have a close bond, something like Arashi and me, but a normal brotherly bond.

We are close to the safe house so we decided to walk the rest of the way. That way Bruce can get a few more moments of relaxation in before we face Dante.

"This is the safe house?" Bruce said looking around us at all the trees.

"No. we are close so we can walk the rest of the way so you can enjoy nature for a few more minutes." Arashi said laughing at what it looks like they all thought the safe house was.

"You thought we were staying in trees." I said laughing

with Arashi as I saw the look on their faces when we
stopped.

"I didn't know what to expect." Bruce said as he
picked a flower out the grass.

"We're almost there. It's up straight ahead. You should
be able to see it." I said walking towards the safe
house.

Chapter Three

We arrived to the safe house to an angry Dante. He was pacing back and forth cursing to himself. It would be scary if he didn't look so much like an angel. Instead he just looked anxious. He noticed we were back with more bodies then we left with. The other's presence did not distract him from getting his anger off his chest.

"You locked me in here." Dante said with furious eyes aimed at both me and Arashi.

"It's a safe house. What part of to keep you safe did you not understand? We turned the alarm on before we left." Arashi said disregarding his attitude.

"It is my decision whether or not I need to be kept safe not yours." Dante snapped

"This safe house is not to protect you. It's to protect

us. Don't assume to think we care about you." Arashi snapped. If Dante push the subject any more he's in for one hell of a beating.

"Not to disrupt the argument but Dante how did you know you were locked in if you didn't try to leave in the first place? You don't even know where you are." I asked curious of why he wanted out.

"I just wanted to step outside for a moment. Is it a crime to want some fresh air?"

"No but you wouldn't be this angry if it was that simple. You want to leave?" I asked. I already believed he was hiding something. Now he's really feeding my assumption.

"I told you I wasn't trying to leave. I just needed some air." Dante was starting to notice our suspicion and started to pay attention to our new guest.

There were more questions to be asked. We needed to find out how everybody in this room fit into the puzzle before we figure out what exactly Dante is hiding. As much as I wanted to grill or possibly torture it out of Dante I decided to play nice until he proves to be no use to us.

I left the room to gather some snacks from the kitchen just in case someone had the munchies like me. I love my junk food especially when I get upset. It's my form of relaxation. When I came back into the living room everyone was calmer. Nathaniel and Joel were speaking amongst themselves in the corner. Bruce set on the couch in front of Dante observing him. Arashi was in the kitchen looking for real food.

"I have some snacks if anyone is interested." I announced as I set them on the table.

"Really Adena. Snacks?" Arashi said detesting junk food.

"What? You don't have to eat it."

"They may want real food. It's been a long day. I sure do." Arashi said while digging in the fridge.

"They can have whatever they want. I'm just offering."

"Adena I would like some please." Joel said coming to the table.

"Of course. No need to ask, just get whatever you want."

"Thank you." Joel said with a low smile on his face.

"No, thank you. It's nice to know somebody other

than me likes junk." I said with a smile on my face. Joel smile widen and that was the first time I really saw him. When he smiles it really shows how gorgeous he is. He went back near the corner to stand by Nathaniel. Something bad must have happened to them for him to get that scar on his face. I can't imagine what or who would want to hurt them. Maybe when they get to know us they will share their story.

"I would like some to." Nathaniel said.

"Then please help yourself. Why don't you come over here and sit with us?" I asked trying to make them feel comfortable.

"We apologize. We are just use to it being just us. We will join you." Nathaniel said as him and Joel came to join us on the couch.

"No apologies needed. Arashi and I are the same way so we understand what you mean." I said.

"Arashi are you going to join us?" I asked knowing she's still looking for food.

"This sucks. We really need to get some food for this place. I thought we already did." Arashi came in the living room fussing since the food was gone."

"We did have food here. Did you forget we had a house guest while we were out?" I said seeing that she forgot we left Dante here.

"We didn't leave him here for a year. It was only a day." Arashi snapped looking from me to Dante.

"I guess were even for me being stuck here." Dante said to Arashi still holding on to his grudge.

"How about next time we put you in a dungeon and see if that's more suited for you." Arashi snapped back at Dante.

Dante got up like he was going to attack Arashi. Arashi smiled waiting for him to strike. As Dante got ready to approach Arashi I jumped in the middle of them to stop them before it got ugly.

"Can you both stop going at it for one minute while we find out who are real enemies are?" I was tired and needed some rest from this long day. All I want to do is find out what Rin is up to and why Sensei Arobi hide who we are in a scroll.

"He asked for it." Arashi said eyeing Dante with a teasing smile.

"Just calm down and have a seat so we can figure out

what's going on." I waited for them to sit down before we started to talk. Both being so stubborn took their precious time. Dante waiting on Arashi and Arashi just staring at Dante. I looked at Arashi and mentally asked her to sit down. There's something more serious going on than your bickering with Dante. She gave me a grave look and sat down.

"Nathaniel can you tell us when you and Joel first learned of your abilities?" I asked.

Nathaniel nodded and proceeded to tell us his story until he was interrupted by Dante.

"What abilities?" Dante asked.

"He was about to tell us before you interrupted him." I said giving Dante an irritated look.

"Arobi didn't say anything about more of us." Dante said.

"How would you know that if you haven't read the scrolls?" Arashi asked.

"My father told me that grandfather would have put it in the scrolls if there were others like you." Dante snapped back at Arashi.

"Clearly your father is holding information back from

you Dante." I said as I turned my attention back to Nathaniel and Joel."

"Nathaniel please go ahead."

"My brother and I never meet our real parents. We were raised in the system but managed to always stay together. Moving from home to home has always been difficult seeing that no one wanted to take two boys. The older we got the harder it was to find a family but someone eventually took us in. It was a married couple who couldn't have kids of their own but wanted boys. We fit the profile perfectly. When we first meet them at the home they were real nice people. They looked as if they had a lot of money so we figured they were wealthy. The fact that they would take a chance with us was a blessing after all the rejects. When they finally got us home everything started to change after that first week.

They hosted a welcoming party for us to introduce us to their family as their sons. The house was amazing and huge. Nothing we have ever seen before. We were very grateful to the point they could have asked us to do anything. The day of the party they took us to the store to buy us some new suits for the party. They said to us that we are a part of the family now and had to play the role in holding up their reputation. For us that was no problem being that it was better than where we came from. So we did as they asked and played the role, but for us it was real. We felt like we had found a good home and were happy.

We mingled with our new family as our new parents introduced us to them. Everybody was nice and accepted us. As the party ended, the family was starting to leave and handed Joel and I envelopes saying 'make sure you use it wisely'. We just smiled and said thank you as they left. When everyone was gone Joel and I went to our room and opened the envelopes to see what was in them. They all had checks for $10,000.00 and more. Before we can register what was going on our parents walked in and took the envelopes saying we will take care of this, goodnight. I asked mother what was the checks for and she said how else you think we are able to live this fabulous life. Then she told us to get some rest because we were leaving in the morning. Joel asked her where we were going and she said home silly then left closing the door behind her.

I didn't want to jump to any assumptions so I did as she said and went to sleep. We were lucky to have a home and didn't want to mess that up our first day asking questions about something that turned out to be nothing.

We were woken up by mother telling us to get our clothes on, grab our things and meet them outside at the car. We got up and did as she said. When we finally made it outside we put our things in the truck and got in the car. Things still seemed to be going good. Our parents were happy, we made it through the first day and there was no sign of any major problems.

We drove for about eight hours before we made it here to the south side of Chicago. We pulled up to a nice two story family home. It was your average home nothing too fancy that will stand out. I was happy about that seeing that it will be easier for us to blend in. We unloaded the car and took everything in the house. When we were done our parents gave us a tour of the house. There was a large living room with basic black furniture. The Dining room was connected to the front room but also a nice side with a long cherry wood table. We made a left through the dining room entrance that leads to a hallway with two rooms. One on the left, one on the right and a bathroom in middle. This is where our parents slept in the room at the far right of the hall. The other room had a basic setup consisting of a bed, dresser, TV and an open closet. The bedroom was empty so we assumed it was one of ours. When we left that area we went back through the dining room into the kitchen. This was a full kitchen and very spacious. It leads to another dining like area with a view of *the back yard.*

The windows were wide. Like looking out into the ocean. We made a left to another part of the kitchen that lead to a huge pantry. The house was much bigger than what it looked like on the outside. When we kept going it lead to stairs for the back door or you can keep going down to a door that was for the basement.

We Came back up and went through the kitchen up the stairs to run into the first room on the right. This room was spacious as well and windows wide so that the view outside was perfect. My new mother told me this was my room. I was more than happy so I set my bags down and turned and looked at mother saying thank you. We than went out my room straight down the hall to another room. This room was bigger than mine with lots and lots of space. This was Joel room. I didn't think anything of it. I was just as happy for him as I was when I saw my room. Joel was excited. This was our first time ever having separate rooms but we were happier knowing we were right down the hall from each other.

They left us alone to get settled in. We unpacked our things and start putting them up and decorating our rooms to make them feel like home. We couldn't asked for anything more. Living in a nice home still together was all we wished for.

As the days passed we were enrolled in school at Percy Lavon Julian located on 103rd and Elizabeth. It turned out to be a nice school. We blended in and made a lot of friends. I was a junior and Joel a sophomore. We did well in school and we were normal happy kids.

Things started to change a little when I decided to join the football team. I started to notice how much faster and stronger I was. It wasn't to the full speed that I have now so I was still able to blend. I was well rounded enough to play both defense and offense. Coach and the rest of the team were happy that our winning streak improved gravely. I had a future in football and was happy until I came home from practice earlier to find mother on the floor and Joel pinned against the wall by father. I immediately dropped my bags and threw father off Joel asking what was going on. Father said "Joel threw your mother on the floor when she was just being nice to him". It already didn't sound right to me being that I know Joel and he wouldn't hurt anybody. I asked Joel is it true and he just looked at me and said no. Father started snapping saying you lucky I didn't send you back to that home; you better start showing us your gratitude for taking both you in. Father than grabbed mother off the floor and they left out of Joel room closing the door.

"Joel what happened?" I asked trying to figure out what was going on.

"She was coming on to me Nathaniel. No mother is that nice." He said with his face twisted in anger.

"What do you mean Joel? What did she do for you to throw her on the floor?"

"She came into my room with some blinds saying she wanted me to help her put them up to keep all the sun from coming in the room. I told her it was fine I like it when the sun comes in. she told me to put them up anyway just in case I change my mind then I can just close the blinds so I did as she asked. I grabbed the blinds from her and put them up. When I was done she said nice job you're going to be very handy around here. I said thank you. She smiled at me walking towards me saying I get very lonely here sometimes when I'm all alone that's why I wanted boys so I can feel safe while your father is gone.

She asked me do I think I can keep her safe from anything so I said I can try my best. She walked around me and put her arms around me like she was giving me a hug than her hands slid down to my dick and I grabbed her hand and I swear I just meant to move her hand off me not throw her across the room.

Nathaniel you have to believe me."

"Joel I believe you. This is your first time noticing your strength?"

"Yes why you ask?"

"I started noticing I was stronger than everybody else when I joined the football team. It triggers my angry side and I lose control for a second like you did."

"What does this mean Nathaniel?"

"I don't know, but we need to find out so I want you to go downstairs and apologize until we figure out what our next move is."

"I don't want to be near her."

"I know. Just give me a couple days okay?"

"Yea."

Joel and I went downstairs so that he can apologize to mother. Mother was in her room whispering something in father's ear. When they saw us father got up angry saying to Joel you came down here to hurt your mother some more. I went in front of Joel blocking father's view of him stating that Joel came to apologize. He didn't mean to hurt mother.

"Well talk up boy." Father said.

Joel looked at me and I nodded for him to go ahead.

"Mother I'm sorry I hurt you it wasn't my intention." Joel said trying to sound like he meant it.

"Well you did." Mother said.

"I'm sorry." Joel apologized again.

"Apology accepted. Don't let it happen again." Mother said.

Joel nodded and we left the room. We went back to our rooms to figure out what we will do next. We decided to play it out for as long as we can. I was turning 18 next year and we will be able to leave freely without going back into the system.

Things stayed cool for a while. Mother and father wouldn't bother us and we wouldn't bother them. We stayed invisible only doing what we had to not to attract attention to ourselves. I quit the football team just in case something was to happen again. Even though everything has been cool I wasn't taking that chance again. Me and Joel went to school together and came home together.

Just like any other Friday we dreaded having to spend a whole weekend in the house. Fridays was father's poker night at the house. We came home from school and father had already started playing with his friends. Joel and I went straight to our rooms so we can stay out the way. Father called me downstairs so I went to see what he wanted.

CONFOUND

"*Nathaniel go to the store and get some more snacks for us.*"
Father said.

"*Where's mother?*" *I asked*

"*She went out. She won't be back till later.*"

"*Ok. What kind of snacks you'll want?*" *I asked looking around the table.*

"*Some chips and dips. O and bring some root beer to.*" *Father said.*

I took the money from father and headed out the door. I didn't have Joel to come with me because the store was right up the street and mother wasn't home yet. I figured there was nothing to worry about. When I made it home father and his friends was no longer in the living room. I went to the kitchen to put the snacks up until they got back and that's when I heard father screaming hold him down don't let him go.

I went to run up the stairs but with a thought I was there standing in Joel room. There was no time to think father friends had Joel pinned down while father burned Joel face with an old steal iron rod. With a flash I threw everybody off Joel picking him up off the floor. I was furious as I asked Joel was he okay. He looked at me different almost as if he was scared when he answered. My back was still turned to father when he said that boy is going to pay for hurting his mother and if you get in my way you will too boy. I turned around to face father and said to him if you even look at Joel again I will make sure it will be the last sight you ever see. Father and his friends fell back screaming his eyes and then they all ran out the room and left. When I turned back to Joel he was still standing in the same spot frozen like he seen a ghost.

"Joel are you sure you ok?" I asked calming myself.

"Yes I am. Are you?" Joel asked me still frozen in place.

"Yes why you ask?"

"Your eyes turned grey. Full blown grey Nathaniel" Joel was moving towards me when my eyes went back to normal.

"I don't know what's going on with me." I said to Joel as I set down taking in the whole situation.

"That's when I first learned of my abilities and had to find out who our birth parents were." Nathaniel said when he finished his story.

"Did you ever find out who your parents were?" Arashi asked.

"Yes. We went back to the home we were originally placed at when we were babies and found out that our mother died shortly after giving birth to Joel. There was nothing on who our father was or if he is still alive." Nathaniel explained with a look of confusion on his face.

"How did you learn how to control your abilities? I ask because there's no sense of anger in you at all." I asked curious of what happened after they found out about their parents.

"After we found out about our parents we went to find someone to teach us how to control our anger. We found Sensei Gin. We told him everything and he agreed to train us. He taught us how not to let our abilities control us." Nathaniel said.

"I know Sensei Gin." Bruce said.

"How?" I turned to look at Bruce when he hesitated to answer the question.

"He is Arobi's brother." Bruce looked up and said. We all looked at Bruce in astonishment. It was a statement neither of us expected. The silence between us was more shock than anything. I was lost in thought.

"Arobi never mentioned a brother to us." Arashi jumped up and said.

"I'm the only one who knew. I sent him a letter when Arobi died to let him know but I never heard back from him." Bruce looked as if he was trying to figure something out at the same time he was telling us about Gin.

"Nathaniel where is Sensei Gin now?" I asked.

"He died February 14, 1998." Nathaniel said.

"That's the same day Sensei Arobi died." I said staring into Nathaniel eyes.

"What does this mean?" We all looked at Bruce for answers.

"It means that you really need to get them scrolls." Bruce said.

"Joel when we were in the street earlier I sensed your strength but not that you have abilities. Do you have any?" I asked looking at Joel.

"No. I only have strength and speed." Joel said.

"That means you and Dante are in the same boat." Arashi said looking back and forth from Joel and Dante.

Joel and Dante shared a look between each other not understanding what this mean. They both are the same as us in some way but don't share our abilities. Finding the scrolls will be the only way to find out. The question is what is it that Dante don't want us to find out.

"Dante it is time for you to tell us what it is you're trying to keep from us." I said looking at Dante not taking my eyes off him.

"What are you talking about?" Dante asked.

"I sensed it when we first met. There's something you're not telling us. What is it?" I gave him a serious look letting him know I won't ask again.

Dante stood there for a minute looking at us trying to figure out his best move. He knew there was no way out. He was no match for me, Arashi, Nathaniel or Joel. When he finally realized he was in over his head he sat down in silence for a minute before he spoke.

"My father despised grandfather for loving you more than him. That's why he closed the dojo. The day he came to take me away he found some of grandfather's scrolls and knew of your abilities then. He made a big scene about me being his son and that I should be with him when all he wanted was to hurt grandfather any way he can. He didn't care about me then and he don't care about me now. He tortured me for years trying to get information out of me about you. I didn't know much about you then. All I knew was that we trained together and you were stronger than me somehow. I never saw you actually use your abilities. Father didn't believe me he beat me every day all day until I finally made up something and told him. After that he started training me to defeat you. I learned how to control my temper and hide my abilities from him until I got old enough to leave. The last time I talked to my father he had already put a bounty out for you. When I confronted him he told me when the time come's I better be ready. I refused to be a part of it. I told him grandfather would not approve of his actions. He laughed and said 'where is your grandfather now' and then he attacked me. That's when I first used my true strength on him. He looked surprised and disgusted at the same time. He told me I will suffer the same death as you will. I smiled at him telling him to give it his best shot. As mad and as hurt as I was I wasn't going to let him see he got to me. I left and came here to find you before anyone else can. I did but barely. I need to know what's in those scrolls just as much as you do. Grandfather never told me who my mother is and my father won't tell me."

"Why wouldn't you just tell us that? Why make it seem like you were working with your father?" I asked furious that he would lead us on with a lie.

"You and Arashi have no idea how much danger you're in. I found you because you are careless with your information and you need to be more cautious. I don't need your sympathy or cockiness. I need you to recognize how much shit you're in. I might not be much of a threat to you but others are. Nathaniel could have been an enemy and you weren't prepared for him. You went in like it's impossible for you to die." Dante snapped back.

"So cute. He cares about us." Arashi said teasing Dante.

"Arashi cool it for a minute." I said.

"Dante I understand your concern but letting us go in blind is not good either." I calmed down and talked to Dante showing him that I appreciate his help.

"I was going to tell you when we were safe. I didn't think that I will be locked in here all day." Dante said.

"Stop being a baby we brought you here to keep you safe. We knew you were keeping something from us and still took a chance." Arashi said.

"That's my point you still took a chance not knowing if I was setting you up." Dante said to Arashi.

"Ok we get it. Dante you have to realize you're underestimating us a lot. You know as much about us as we know of you." I said trying to defuse the situation.

"Your right. I'm sorry for not telling you but you have to promise to be more cautious." Dante looked into my eyes pleading with me to be more careful.

"Okay we promise." I agreed.

Things were starting to come together. Now that we knew more about each of our situation we can work on getting the scrolls. It was a good start but I wasn't sure I wanted to walk down this road. I want to know where we came from but I'm not sure if it will change much about us.

I'm happy knowing Sensei Arobi loved us as his own. I

don't want to be selfish towards the others finding out the truth, I'm just not sure if I want to know for myself. Our parents left us and never came back. What excuse can make up for that in any way? Me and Arashi use to think about our parents all the time. We wanted nothing more but to know them. What they looked like, there personalities, whether they were happy together and why not take us with them. As time passed it didn't matter anymore. We have each other and that's all that matter. No one will break our bond. Not even Rin. For Arashi and the others I will get those scrolls and hope for a happy ending.

It was late when we decided to get some rest and figure out the rest in the morning. Arashi showed Bruce and Dante where they will be sleeping and I took Nathaniel and Joel to their rooms. We had to stick together. I asked them if they wanted separate rooms or to stay together. Nathaniel said "whatever you can accommodate will be fine." I took them to separate rooms that were joined together by a bathroom. I showed them where everything was just in case they needed something extra. Joel nodded and went to his room to get some rest. Nathaniel stood there for a minute staring at me.

"What?" I asked getting nervous from his gaze lingering on me.

"I'm sorry I didn't mean to make you uncomfortable." Nathaniel said. He looked at me with passion and lust in his eyes. His beauty is of a God. Perfection no matter which way you looked at him. Now I was the one staring. I can't deny the attraction I have for him. The need to be with him. I wanted to yield to him and let him live out his fantasies with me. I froze when Nathaniel was suddenly standing in front of me taking a gentle finger to stroke the side of my face.

"Such beauty." Nathaniel said catching my eyes.

"Thanks." I said moving away from Nathaniel to catch my breath he had just stolen away from me.

"Please, don't go. Adena I never felt this connection for anybody before. I know you feel it to, I see how hard it is for you to resist." Nathaniel said coming towards me again taking his hands along the curves of my body, learning me with just a touch.

He was right. It is hard for me to resist him. I never

wanted anyone more than I wanted him. It felt like we were meant to be. We have to indulge ourselves in this pleasure or lose it forever. I yielded to him, letting him feel me up, moaning in need. He walked behind me lifting my arms to wrap around his neck, and then moving his hands slowly down my neck until he reached my breast. His warm hands glided over my breast and kept going till he reached the end of my shirt.

He began lifting my shirt up never taking his hands off my body but used a slow motion with his hands moving up my stomach and landing under my breast cupping them firmly giving them a deep massage. I moaned letting my head fall back unto him, locking my arms around him.

He began to move his hand down my stomach and reached into my pants, creeping his fingers in like he was a spider going to get his prey. He reached my clit and took his index finger and thumb to gently squeeze it over and over again. I cried out from the pleasure spreading my legs even more.

"Yes let me please you." Nathaniel said listening to me

moan and cry out. I was lost in the pleasure he was giving me. I wanted more of him. Wanted him to fuck me and take my mind off of today. He had me, I was all his in that moment.

"What I want to do to you." Nathaniel said bringing me back to reality. I suddenly thought of Quentin and broke the connection.

"I can't do this." I said running out the room trying to get as far away as I could.

"Wait, Adena." I heard Nathaniel call out to me but it was too late I was already gone.

I needed some air so I ran through the forest wanting to clear my head. I couldn't, all I could think about was how ashamed I was for giving myself to Nathaniel. How I completely lost myself forgetting about Quentin.

The thoughts just kept running in my head playing over and over again. I stopped running collapsing to my knees trying to cry my hormones away. In that moment Nathaniel voice played in my head. "*What I want to do to you*", I wanted him and needed him like he was it for me. My breast still ached from his touch. My body trembled for pleasure instead of shaking from disappointment. I needed to get away. I got up to go to Quentin but was suddenly stopped by Arashi.

"It's ok Adena. You did nothing wrong." Arashi said trying to comfort me.

"I have to go apologize to Quentin. I can't believe I…….." I started to say until Arashi cut me off.

"You can't believe you did what? Run from a handsome man while in need." Arashi said laughing.

"This is not funny Arashi. I'm very serious." I said mad that Arashi found a way to make a joke.

"I'm just saying. You did nothing wrong. You gave in a little to your hormones. So what. Yes you feel wrong for forgetting about Quentin for 5 minutes but who is it really going to make feel better by you telling him that. Not him. You will feel better once you cleared your conscious but when you see his face both of your hearts will be broken. Do you want that instead?" Arashi said.

"No. you're right. Thank you Arashi." I gave Arashi a hug for stopping me from doing something I would have regretted.

"No problem, just don't go all mushy on me okay?"
Arashi said leading the way back to the safe house.

"Yea, yea, yea." I said laughing at Arashi.

We started walking towards the safe house and I
noticed that Arashi has on lingerie. I know Arashi likes
to look sexy at all times but she's a no underwear gal.
When Arashi wear lingerie it means she's planning on
having a good time.

"Um Arashi. Why are you in Lingerie? Are you about
to go somewhere?" I asked looking suspicious

"No. I decided to wear something to bed seeing that
we have company." Arashi said trying not to look back
at me.

I was about to tell Arashi I know she's lying due to the
fact she doesn't care who sees her goodies until she
start having flash backs of her night before she came
to stop me.

"Arashi are you crazy you were having sex with Joel?"
I said hollering at a low tone.

"Will you be quiet? That's something you could have
asked in thought Adena." Arashi said.

"When do you care about people knowing if you're

having sex or not?" I asked not letting her off the subject.

"I don't. Joel doesn't want any attention on him." Arashi said

I laughed knowing that it has to be killing Arashi to hold her actions back. I respected Joel wishes and continued having our conversation in thought.

Chapter Four

I was woken by the sun hitting my face in the
morning. I never close my blinds since I enjoy the
beauty of nature. I laid there for a minute taking in the
silence for a moment. When I got up I went to the
bathroom to wash my face and brush my teeth like any
other day. I was relaxed considering last night. It was
like a long forgotten dream. I felt as if I was walking
on thin air, very calm and collective. I smiled feeling
unbelievably free until I stepped back into my room. I
was surprised to see Nathaniel waiting and smiling
from watching me enjoy each step I made. I jumped,
another unusual reaction being that I would have
attacked first and ask question later.

"What are you doing in my room?" I asked still
surprised by my reaction to him.

"I didn't mean to scare you. I just wanted to apologize for last night." Nathaniel said trying to keep his distance from me but not succeeding.

"It's ok. I don't blame you for my reaction." I said walking to my closet to get a robe. I never been modest before but for some reason I'm acting as a shy school girl.

"Are you sure? People seem to bring out there inner desires or fears around me." Nathaniel said moving away from me unsure what his approach should be.

"What do you mean Nathaniel? Why am I so different when I'm around you alone?" I asked wanting to know more of what's triggering our attraction for each other.

"I have the ability to pull people inner desires out of them but it does not always work in my favor. If I do anything to make you uncomfortable or fearful of me than you desires turn into your greatest fear. I can control it but it back fires when my own desires are mixed in." Nathaniel tried to explain.

"So you were trying to seduce me with your abilities last night?" I asked

"No I was letting you feel my desires for you. Your

reaction was an enhancement of your own desires. I cannot place the feeling, I can only enhance it." Nathaniel said smiling once again.

"You can stop smiling I don't feel anything for you Nathaniel. You must have tapped into my feelings for Quentin." I explained to Nathaniel trying more so to convince myself then him.

"I know this is a lot to take in but I felt how much you wanted me when we were on the road. Your first instinct was to attack me but you never tried to hurt me. You knew then that you can trust me and my brother." Nathaniel said looking into my eyes, holding me there to rethink the situation. He was right I didn't want to hurt him but it was only because I didn't believe they wanted to hurt us. I knew he and his brother wasn't a threat to us.

"I didn't think you or Joel was a threat. That is the only reason I did not harm you." I said turning away from Nathaniel.

"Well my apologies. It won't happen again. Not unless you want it to." Nathaniel said giving me one last glance before he walked out my room.

I laid on the bed staring at the ceiling. I just wanted to relax and clear my mind. Just like everything else in my life it's not that simple. Nathaniel words kept playing over in my head *"not unless you want it to"*. Yes I wanted to and it wasn't because of his abilities influence on me. It was a natural feeling like he was Jason playing my lyrics. I want him as much as I want Quentin but deep down I truly believe Quentin is my soul mate. I can't help but ask myself what if Nathaniel ended up changing that. What will happen if I gave in to him? I broke free of my obsessive thinking and started to get dress so I can join the others. Everyone was up and conversing among themselves while waiting to eat breakfast. I took my time going down the stairs so I could take a deep breath and get rid of the jitters I suddenly have. I thought of my last night with Quentin and everything else disappeared. I was at peace with a smile bright on my face. I walked over to the kitchen and start helping with breakfast.

"Adena who do you think is better Achilles or Hercules?" Bruce asked me putting me in the middle of his conversation with Dante.

"I would have to say Achilles." I answered agreeing with Dante.

"How could you say that Adena? You know Hercules fought for good and Achilles fought for himself." Bruce said surprised by my answer.

"That's why Bruce. Hercules spent his time protecting others while Achilles served himself. I admire his freedom that's all." I explained to Bruce. In real life I value Hercules beliefs but deep down I crave Achilles freedom.

"I understand." Bruce said. He saw how much I wanted it for myself and struggled to accept who or what I might be.

I took over the plate of Pancakes Bruce just finished and walked them over to the dining table where Arashi and Joel was finishing setting up the plates, napkins, forks, spoons and knives. It was like watching the overly popular high school girl fall for the school bad ass. It made me laugh. Arashi has never reframed herself from getting what she wants. She must really like the challenge. Joel took quick looks at Arashi as she maneuvered her body in sexy ways while setting the table to get him going. She was rewriting the story of snow white and the huntsman seducing him every chance she got.

We all sat at the table so that we can eat breakfast. Arashi sitting across from Joel, Nathaniel across from me and Dante across from Bruce. We looked like one big happy family even though we only known each other for a second. We passed the food around the table making our plates and eating in silence. The one thing we all had in common was that we enjoy the lack of conversation while eating. After we were done Joel and Arashi washed the dishes.

We gathered in the living room to go over our plan for getting the scrolls. Even though Arashi and I know the ins and outs of Arobi dojo we did not know all of the secret passage ways. We needed to figure out how to get in without being noticed. Rin is expecting us and would have traps set to catch us. The real question is can he exactly harm us. Arashi and I have never been weakened or hurt by anything manmade before but considering Rin knows about us, then he must have a way to capture us.

"I know my father will be expecting us, it won't be long before they figure out we're in." Dante said pacing back and forth.

"That's true but your father may not be expecting us to just walk in." Arashi said stopping Dante from pacing.

"She may have a point Dante. Rin is too stubborn to think of the obvious." Bruce said remembering back when Rin was younger.

"I want him to see us coming since he put a bounty out on us." Arashi said wanting to make an entrance.

"Just walking in will surely take him by surprise." I said looking at Nathaniel but mentally saying it to Arashi.

"Yes. That's a reaction I would like to see." Arashi agreed reading my thoughts.

"Hello can you speak to the rest of us who can't read your mind." Dante asked irritated by our connection.

"How did you know we can hear each other thoughts?" I asked Dante seeing we never told him.

"It's obvious when you and Arashi stare at each other nodding at unspoken questions. It's also obvious when you start talking about something then stop when someone enter the room but never take your eyes off each other." Dante explained.

"You pay attention, that's good." Bruce said to Dante.

"Yes it is." Arashi said.

"He put a bounty out for us so why not let Nathaniel and Joel walk us straight to him. On the way out Nathaniel and Joel can take out whatever man Rin have lingering around, while Bruce get Arobi hidden scroll from the dojo and you get the scrolls your father have." I said giving them a ruff run down of my plan. We can figure out exact details later.

"How will you and Arashi get out?" Dante asked.

"We will fight our way out when it's clear you all got out safely." I said making it sound simple. It is crazy to think Rin won't be able to keep us locked up but I have confidence that Rin doesn't know as much about us as he thinks.

"You can't be sure that you and Arashi will make it out." Dante said.

"He is right Adena. You don't know what all Rin knows about you or what your weakness are." Bruce said surprised that I would want to go in blindsided.

"I know but all we can do is guess what's up his sleeve just like all he can do is guess what's up ours. Everything he will try to detain us with is based on what he has done to Dante. He knows Dante have some of our strengths and speed but he doesn't know we don't have the same weakness. We play the part and strike when he thinks he has us." I explained.

"How can you be sure it will work?" Nathaniel asked with a look of concern on his face. You can tell he's playing the scenario in his head as I explained it and mixed it in with us getting caught.

"It all depends on how much information is on the bounty or we're screwed." I said looking into Nathaniel eyes.

"Why would that matter?" Dante asked.

"If he did not include a way to capture them than he knows it's impossible and is using them as bate to catch others. In the meantime leaving a bounty for Nathaniel and Joel as well." Bruce explained to Dante while meditating on the floor.

"If we walk them straight in to him he will know that there was only two ways we caught her. Either we also have abilities or they came voluntary." Nathaniel said shifting his eyes to Joel.

"So either way we look at it we're being set up." Dante said.

"Yes. Nathaniel do you still have the bounty on us?" I asked.

"I do but it is at home." Nathaniel said.

"It's time to take a trip." I said ready to get out the safe house.

"Do we all need to go?" Bruce asked enjoying his peace here.

"No. Bruce you can stay. We have several things to do so we all can split up and meet back at the road before the forest." I said.

"What all is there to do besides get the bounty?" Dante asked.

"Hello we need food and more clothes." Arashi said irritated by Dante 21 questions.

"We're going to split up into groups." I said.

"Good I'll take Joel." Arashi said smiling seductively at the idea of being alone with Joel.

"We have to get clothes Arashi don't you think he

want to pick his own clothes." I said angry at Arashi for thinking only of sex.

"Nathaniel could grab his clothes just like I can get yours." Arashi snapped back at me with big eyes and a fake smile on her face.

"Okay and what am I going to do because I'm not staying here again." Dante asked.

"You can go with Arashi and Joel to make sure they stay on track." I said returning the fake smile to Arashi.

"No he can go to the grocery store and get food for the safe house." Arashi said dropping her smile.

"Grocery store. I don't know what to get." Dante said

"I will make a list." Bruce said as he got paper and a pen to start jotting things down.

"Great." Dante said not happy with his task.

"I will go with you to make sure you get everything." Bruce said seeing the uneasy look on Dante's face.

"Are you sure Bruce? If you want to stay I can go to the store and Dante can join Nathaniel." I asked trying to avoid being alone with Nathaniel.

"No it is fine. I will go." Bruce said.

"Ok let's head out the door." I said.

The plan was crappie but I wanted to get it over with. The only thing that mattered at this point is finding out who we are. I went to my room to put my shoes on and grab my jacket. I went in the bathroom to make sure my hair was okay and ended up staring at myself in the mirror. I noticed the perfection in my face. I never had facial problems even when going through puberty. My beauty has remained untouched. I never really aged. I always considered myself to be average trying to convince myself I was no different from others by being invisible.

When I stared at the mirror I saw the roundness of my cheeks, the brightness in my eyes, and the smoothness of my skin and how even my skin tone was. I looked like an adult in a teenage body.

It was time to go. We are going to move one step closer to finding out what or who we are. I left the bathroom and went downstairs to meet everybody else. They were waiting for me at the door wandering what took so long.

"Sorry I'm ready." I said uncomfortable with all eyes

being on me.

"Ok let's go." Arashi said leading us out the door.

Chapter Five

We made it to the city and split up like we planned. Nathaniel and I headed to his place. He insisted on taking a cab when I said it will be cheaper to take the bus.

"Where do you stay anyway?" I asked not knowing what to expect.

"Why? Are you scared I will trap you in and do nasty things to you?" Nathaniel smiled at me waiting for me to deny his accusation.

"I'm not worried I was just asking." I said laughing at him for thinking he can.

"Have you admitted to yourself that you're attracted to me yet?" Nathaniel asked feeling way to confident about himself.

"I never said you weren't attractive." I said not really

answering the question.

"That's not what I asked you but I'll let it go." Nathaniel said as he instructed the driver where to go.

"You live downtown?" I said surprised since he seemed like a stay to himself type of guy.

"Yes. Just because I don't like attention doesn't mean I don't like luxury." It didn't take that long to get to Nathaniel's place. The traffic wasn't that bad considering Chicago unpredictable traffic on the express ways. When we finally made it to Nathaniel's place he paid the driver and got out the cab.

He held the door open for me and helped me out the cab as I took in where he lives. He stayed in the south loop at eight east Ninth Street in the Astoria Tower. This place is beautiful and looked very luxurious. I wonder what he does to be able to afford such a nice place. We were greeted by the concierge as we walked in the building. He bowed his head and acknowledged Nathaniel as sir. Nathaniel nodded and led the way to his place. We entered the elevator and I watched him press floor thirty that leads to the penthouse.

"Penthouse? You doing it big aren't you?" I asked still

surprised at his style of living.

"It's the best." Nathaniel said with a half-smile on his face.

The elevator stopped on his floor and we went to his place that was absolutely stunning. The first thing I noticed was the floor to ceiling windows. It has the perfect view of Chicago east side. His place is big in size and the way he furnished it made it feel like home. This is another surprise to me. He didn't go for the bachelor look. I took it upon myself to look around his place. It was so beautiful and nicely decorated.

"Make yourself at home." Nathaniel said watching me look around his place with amazement in my eyes.

"Oh I'm sorry. I just can't believe your taste. It's amazing." I said still walking around his place.

"No need to apologize I know my personality doesn't match my taste. Would you like a tour?" Nathaniel asked extending his hand out to me.

"Yes please." I gave him my hand and let him lead the way through his place. The little gesture of holding his hand sent flutters inside me. I felt as if I belonged to him and didn't want to let go.

He began with the living room since we were already there, and then moved to the kitchen. He walked me through showing me as if he is the realtor and he really wanted to sell me this penthouse. If he was the salesman I would have bought it just because of the comfort I felt with him. After he showed me the kitchen we moved on to the den.

Nicely decorated as usual with a long oak wood table. We moved on down the hall into the master bedroom. It is very spacious with a walk in closet, a full bath and another stunning view. We left out his room and went to Joel's room that was similar to Nathaniel's. Everything is the same accept Nathaniel bathroom and closet space was a little bigger. Nothing very noticeable but expected. Last but not least he showed me the other bathroom that's mainly used for guest.

We were finished with the tour so Nathaniel led us back to his room so he can start packing some of his clothes. I walked out on his Terrance from his room and took in the beautiful view. It wasn't long before Nathaniel joined me. I felt his presence as soon as he stepped out on the Terrance.

"We can stay longer if you like." Nathaniel said to me as I closed my eyes and took in the smells from the lake and the breeze from the wind.

"No we have to meet up with the others. I don't want them waiting too long for us." I said and opened my eyes as I turned to face Nathaniel.

He walked over to me grasping my hands and holding my gaze. It gave me a feeling of need for him. I wanted his touch, I wanted to be here with him and everything in my body was fighting me to stay here with him.

"Let's just stay a few more minutes." Nathaniel said as he spent me around and wrapped his arms around me while we looked at the view. It felt good like I've known him forever and he was my safe heaven.

He started to kiss me on my neck softly and slowly making me feel like time had just stopped for us. The feeling was intoxicating giving him leverage on me but I caught myself and moved away from him. I walked back into his room.

"Please I think we should leave." I said ready to get away from this pull we have for each other.

"Don't run from me. Why won't you give in to your feelings for me? I know you want to." Nathaniel said as he walked towards me again.

"Stop! Stay where you are. This is wrong. Yes I feel something for you and I don't know why but I'm in a relationship with someone I love very much. This is wrong on so many levels." I said trying to maintain my distance.

"You can't keep fighting your feelings. It's okay to feel something for more than one person." Nathaniel said making his way to me again.

"It's not ok to be intimate with you." I said walking out his room and back into the living room.

"Yes it is. You can feel it. The attraction we have for each other. It has to be because of who we are. I've never been more attracted to any one like this before. When I'm around you you're the only thing that matters to me besides Joel. Can you explain that?" Nathaniel asked following me back into the living room. Making me think about what he just said.

"No I can't which is more reason to get these scrolls before we do something we regret." I said hoping he would just let it go.

"There won't be any regret on my part. I'll finish getting our things so we can leave." Nathaniel said.

I waited for him in the living room sitting on the couch. I knew it wouldn't take long I just needed to calm my nerves. I took a few deep breaths, closed my eyes and told myself it will all be over soon. I was distracted by someone coming into Nathaniel's place. When he made himself visible he was six feet tall, light skinned with short cut hair. He was dressed in an all-black suit that was tailored made for him. He was average looking nothing really stood out about him. He can easily be mistaken as your average business man. He looked at me with a cocky smile on his face.

"Well not who I expected but a beautiful lady is always a joy to be around." The strange man said walking towards me.

"Seth what are you doing here?" Nathaniel said instantly appearing in the living room.

"Ah Nathaniel I was coming to check and see how things were going for you but I see why you been so occupied." Seth said not taking his eyes off me.

"You could have just called." Nathaniel said adding more aggression to his voice.

"I know but dropping in is much more fulfilling to me." Seth said smiling at Nathaniel.

"Is there a problem?" I asked not liking the tone I hear in Nathaniel's voice.

"No just a misunderstanding. Right Nathaniel?" Seth said as he looked back and forth from me to Nathaniel.

"Well maybe I can help clear it up." I said to Seth.

Seth smile got even bigger at my words and then he started to laugh. I looked at Nathaniel who wouldn't take his eyes off Seth. It was if he wanted to attack him but for some reason couldn't.

"The only way you can fix the problem is to die Adena." Seth said surprising me with his words. He knew my name.

"And are you going to be the one to kill me?" I asked with a smile. I was interested in how he planned to kill me.

"No Nathaniel is." Seth said watching my face twist in confusion as I looked at Nathaniel now crouched down looking at me ready to attack.

"Nathaniel what are you doing?" I asked pissed that Nathaniel got me to trust him and trapped me.

"There's no need to try to talk him out of it. He had strict orders to kill you on sight. I don't know how you got him to break our agreement. He's always got his mark." Seth said.

"Why would he listen to you?" I snapped at Seth wanting to know what his hold on Nathaniel was.

"I have something he wants. What do you have?" Seth looked at me pleased with his control over Nathaniel.

"Confidence that I will kill you." I said with a vague smile on my face.

"Maybe but not before you. Nathaniel kill her." Seth demanded.

Nathaniel launched at me moving almost faster than a speeding bullet. I blocked his attacked sending him flying across the room. I didn't turn to face him because just the little I knew about Nathaniel told me he's not going to hurt me. Nathaniel is a skilled fighter who would never fight so sloppy. With an instant I was in front of Seth slamming him into the wall.

I heard Nathaniel coming behind me so I moved at the last moment allowing him to crash into Seth. I grabbed Nathaniel throwing him to the other side of the living room. With a blink of the eye I was in front of Nathaniel breaking his legs. I knew he would heel but not in time for me to deal with Seth. I walked backed over to Seth knowing he wouldn't try to run. I lifted him up in the air by his neck squeezing slowly making him grasps for air.

"What do you have on him?" I asked Seth releasing my firm hold on him enough for him to breath.

"I have information on his real mother and I have his real birth certificate." Seth said.

I looked at him in his eyes and held him there trying to control my anger. I felt a surge of power come into me as I spoke to him.

"You have two hours to get the information and give it to us. If I see you again after that I won't hesitate to kill you. You will take the information to a club called the underground located 56 W. Illinois St. and leave it with the bar tender. Two hours or I'm coming for you." I said than dropped him to the floor. He ran out the door as fast as he could, not bothering to look back at me or Nathaniel.

I looked over at Nathaniel who is healed but still sitting in the corner. I knew how bad he felt for having to attack me so I wasn't going to nag him about it.

"Are you ok?" I asked Nathaniel as I walked over and crouched down beside him.

"I'm sorry." Nathaniel said looking into my eyes to show his sincerity.

"I know. Just like I knew you weren't really trying to attack me." I said smiling to make him feel better.

"He doesn't know about me so I didn't want to tip him off." Nathaniel started to explain.

"I think you messed up when you attacked me at full speed." I said drawing it to his attention.

"He knows I'm skilled but he doesn't know of my abilities. He thinks I'm a ninja." He said finally smiling up at me.

"Wow." I said laughing at the thought. It wasn't too farfetched with his training but the speed is pushing it.

"You scared him but he won't give up so easily." Nathaniel said getting up. "I guess we will deal with him when the time comes. We have a lot to find out about ourselves along the way." Nathaniel said.

"Until then can we go before you get any more visitors?" I said urging him to get their things.

"Yes just let me grab the bounty." He said as he went to a safe hidden behind a painting of him and Joel.

We left Nathaniel's place and got in another cab to head back to the meeting spot. I still had to go get Nathaniel's information from the club shortly but I rather go alone. The underground is Quentin's club that he bartends at himself to keep an eye on the place. It would be too weird to walk in there with Nathaniel.

I told the driver to just drive and I will instruct him where to go. He nodded and drove away. We pulled on the express way and headed back to the meet up spot. Nathaniel asked me about the club and wandered why we just didn't go there and wait for Seth to drop off the information he had about his real mother. I told him about Quentin and how weird it would be for him to be there. I told him I didn't feel like explaining him to Quentin seeing that he doesn't know about me. Nathaniel didn't agree with my decision but didn't push the issue.

He warned me that Seth always had tricks up his sleeve and that I should be careful. I agreed as I instructed the cab driver where to go. I didn't want him to take us to the exact spot so I had him stop a little ways before. He was surprised that we wanted to get off on the expressway so I gave him a big tip to take his mind off it. We waited for him to pull off before we headed up the hill to the meeting spot.

Nathaniel and I were having a brief conversation when we made it up the hill until I felt a strong jerk in my body. It was an intense pull and I had no idea where it was coming from but it was painful. I looked at Nathaniel as he came to my aid to try to figure out what was wrong. The pull was internal like someone was trying to rip me inside out. The harder I fought the pull the sharper the pain got.

"What's going on Adena? What's wrong?" Nathaniel said feeling helpless to my cries.

"I don't know something is trying to pull me." I said in agony.

"Fighting it is making the pain worse. You're going to

have to give in to it." He said hovering over me trying not to touch me.

"It hurts either way." I said bending over from the pain.

Nathaniel put his arms around me, telling me to give in to the pull. I didn't want to but I did. I felt my eyes change blood red and instantly me and Nathaniel was in a room standing before Arashi and Joel having sex. The intensity from there pleasure turned Arashi eyes ice blue and as she felt her pleasure, I felt her pain and it brought me here to them. I fought back at the pull and we were back at the meeting spot. Not knowing how to respond to what we just seen. Nathaniel let go of me not understanding what just happened.

"What the hell was that?" Nathaniel said still in shock.

"Some very intense sex." I said looking at Nathaniel.

"That was my brother and your sister." He said walking up to me.

"Yes." I said watching his reaction.

"Where are they?" Nathaniel asked.

"They're at Arashi house in Willow Brook." I answered.

"Wow." Nathaniel said sitting on the ground.

"Yea nice house huh?" I said knowing that's not what he meant.

"Did you feel that? I can feel their arousal." Nathaniel said.

"You were feeling Joel arousal and I was feeling Arashi's twisted satisfaction of sex." I explained trying to shake the memory.

"Do you and Arashi always pull each other in the middle of sex?" Nathaniel asked.

"No and hopefully that was the last time." I said taking a seat on the ground with Nathaniel.

We sat there for a minute in silence before Bruce and Dante arrived with the groceries. Bruce was huffing and puffing from the climb up the hill while Dante set the bags down and had a seat.

I was still stuck in Arashi pull but it had died down a lot. The only problem now was the images and lingering feelings Arashi was having towards the end. This is a sick way to be connected I thought to myself. When Arashi responded to my thought it really surprised me.

"Were you watching us?"

"More like you pulled me in and I took Nathaniel and we had to see you and Joel in action."

"OMG I can't believe you both were watching."

"Trust me that was something we didn't want to see but your pull was so damn strong I had to give in to it and I ended up there seeing you two."

"We really need to work on this bond."

"I agree with that. When did you start to care about being modest though?"

"I don't know. It's different with Joel. I feel like I have to."

"Okay we can figure that out later. Get here to the meeting spot we're waiting for you."

"We're on our way."

It didn't take Arashi and Joel long to meet us. When they arrived we made our way through the forest and back to the safe house. When we made it to the house everyone split up. Bruce and Dante went to put the food up as I shared with Arashi what happened at Nathaniel's place. Nathaniel and Joel went to their rooms to put there things up and to have a talk.

Arashi and I got ready to go to the underground so

that I can get Nathaniel papers. It was better this way just in case Seth had something up his sleeve. He shares the same bounty as Nathaniel and doesn't seem like he will give up so easy.

We left the guys home alone while we went to go play in our usual spot. The underground is where I spend time with Quentin and Arashi search for her new playmate. We are known very well here thanks to all the attention Arashi causes.

We always get to the club late seeing that it starts off slow on some days. Everyone who comes here are like night walkers who can't sleep at night. This time we had a mission that only allowed us to go in and get out. When we made it to the club Rick the bouncer let us right in. He was surprised to see us so early in the day.

"You girls too early aren't you?" Rick asked holding the door open for us.

"It's a business stop instead of a pleasure stop." Arashi responded as she usually does when flirting with Rick.

"Too bad. It hasn't been the same without you." Rick said clearly stating how much he missed Arashi.

"I know. Don't worry we'll be back." Arashi said teasing Rick.

"I can't wait." Rick said staring at Arashi's ass as we walked away.

I walked straight to the bar to see Quentin while Arashi mingled with other staff members she knew. When Quentin saw me coming his face lit up with excitement and I couldn't help but to blush. He came from behind the bar to meet me and gave me the biggest hug ever. I can tell he missed me and the feeling is mutual. I know that he will be upset when I tell him I can't stay.

As much as I want to tell him what's going on, I don't want him mixed in with our problems. He is the only person that can take my mind away from reality and just enjoy the moment. All that will change if I have to worry myself about his protection. We walked back over to the bar and before I can mention the papers, he was handing them to me with a smile on his face.

"Thank you." I said holding back another blush from him.

"It's no problem. Why didn't you call and tell me you

were expecting a package?" He asked not really caring about the package and just wanting to hear my voice.

"I would have but it was last minute and I figured I will just show up." I explained holding his gaze.

"If holding a package for you gives me a chance to see you more, than send whatever you want here or better yet my place." Quentin said as he put his hand under my chin lifting my face to give me a kiss.

"Thank you." I said again.

"I have something for you." Quentin said reaching into his pocket to pull out a small gift wrapped box.

"Really? You didn't have to get me anything." I said surprised by the gift.

"It's something I really want you to have, so open it." Quentin said placing it in my hand.

I stared at it for a moment trying to figure out what it was and hoping it wasn't a ring but dying in the inside for it to be a ring. I shook it and twirled it side to side trying to figure out what it was. When I looked up at Quentin he made a hand gesture telling me to hurry and open it. I took the wrapping off and it was a small box that looked like a typical ring box. I took a deep breath and opened the box pulling out a set of keys. I smiled with relief but wasn't sure what the keys belonged to.

"These are the keys to my place so you can just come in instead of knocking." Quentin said waiting on my response.

"Are you sure you want me to have these?" I asked. Seeing that I don't pop up that often and when I do it's always unexpected.

"Yes. Do you want them?" Quentin asked now confused by my reaction.

"Yes I do. I really do thank you." I said smiling and trying to show more of my appreciation.

"Good." Quentin said and leaned over to give me another kiss.

"Thank you again for keeping these paper's for me." I said as I got up to leave.

"You welcome. Wait your leaving already? You just got here." Quentin said with that look of disappointment on his face I always cause when I leave.

"I have to get these papers back. They're very

important to my friend who is patiently waiting for me to return." I explained.

"That makes two of us." Quentin said soaking more into his feeling.

"I'm sorry. I promise you, you will see me soon and I will use my key." I said smiling up at him trying to turn around his mood.

"Don't keep me waiting long Adena." He said pulling me to him to kiss me passionately.

"I won't." I said catching my breath after I lost it with that kiss.

Arashi and I headed out to go back to the safe house. It was time to find out what the bounty had on how to capture us. Also it was time for Nathaniel and Joel to have peace about who their real mother was.

Arashi and I decided to run. It's the only real time we have together since the bounty went out for us. We decided to race all the way there which was pointless seeing that neither one of us ever wins. The fun we get out of trying while tricking and tripping each other as we ran is worth the fun in the end. We jumped, climbed and twisted around everything in the forest like we had just jumped out of the movie Tarzan. We laughed and taunted the forest like two ghost finally set free.

When we made it back to the safe house Bruce had just finished dinner and the smell of a home cooked meal hit us instantly. We ran over to the kitchen to see what Bruce made and he stopped us pleading with us to take a shower. From all the running and playing we smelled just like outdoors which wasn't so pleasant to our new guest. As we went to our rooms to clean ourselves up we heard Bruce fussing about us being like two little girls running and playing in the house. Me and Arashi laughed and went our separate ways.

Chapter Six

After dinner we gathered around to finally look over
the bounty. Nathaniel stretched it out because it is a
long scroll like sheet of paper. It has a picture of both
me and Arashi. He couldn't have known how we look
now so he used the old photos of us when we were
teenagers at the dojo.

We still look exactly the same. Because of his
monitoring of Dante he knew that we would not have
aged as much. The details under our picture are our
names Adena and Arashi trained in Japanese jujitsu
both are a danger to those who come in their path.
With deadly abilities they are an abomination to
mankind. To any person who can capture them there
is a five million dollar bounty when you bring them to
me.

The bounty can only be collected if they are alive. Call this number when you have caught the bounty and I will come to you with cash in my hand. Remember their abilities make them a challenge to catch. The only thing that can trap them is pure iron shackles or anything made of iron. If you catch them, breaking of their bones will prevent them from healing for at least three hours.

"Is that true?" Bruce asked looking at me.

"The pure iron I have no idea but the three hours from breaking our bones no. We heal instantly." I said to Bruce.

"The only way to find out is to try it." Bruce said getting up to find something of iron.

"Bruce is right we need to know what our weakness is before we go in." I said looking at the others.

"Why would he think that this will work?" Arashi asked still looking over the scroll.

"When he had me locked up that's what he used on me and when he broke my bones it took me that long to heal." Dante explained.

"Why did it take you so long to heal?" I asked Dante

being that he healed his self-much faster in the woods when we first met.

"I didn't know much about my strengths then. I wasn't taught how to control them so I was learning in the process. I only tried when no one else was around." Dante explained.

"That means we need to finish your training." Arashi said smiling at Dante. Overly excited about challenging him.

"We need to know where you stand in skill first which mean since you and Joel are of equal strength you will challenge each other." I said looking back and forth from Joel and Dante.

The tension between them was weird. As long as we've been here they have not talked or tried to interact with each other at all. Dante does come off as not trust-worthy but Joel has a keep to himself attitude. If I was just meeting them both I would think that they were natural enemies. I don't know what to think about this training. I am sure we will get exactly what we ask to see from them.

I watched Dante and Joel just stand there and observe

each other with no real facial expressions or intent. Whatever it is between them we need to figure it out. Everybody else headed outside for training as I waited for the staring battle between Joel and Dante to end. Joel looked at me with suspension in his eyes and then back to Dante before finally breaking the connection and heading towards the door. I gestured for Dante to go ahead and I followed behind. This will be very interesting.

Bruce took us through a few warm up exercise to relax our mind and let go of all animosity. Since we didn't have any iron laying around anywhere. We focused on getting in the right head space so we can fight with clarity and not emotion. We can't get blindsided by the people we love or respect.

To get everything going on a good path Arashi and I went first. Usually this wouldn't be good for people who are as close to each other as we are, but we understand battle is battle and our worst enemy can very well be each other.

We faced each other in the open space between the trees where we usually train. I have a basic stands that put me in a position to expect anything. Arashi has more of a Charlie angels stands but don't be mistaken she can't be budged. We charged towards each other coming head on. Arashi went for a low spinning kick as I jumped over her going for a high jump kick. Arashi grabbed my leg spinning me in a full circle before letting me go sending me flying across the forest.

I flipped backwards landing on my feet springing at her full speed landing on her shoulders, throwing her as I flipped backwards landing on my feet. Arashi gripped on to a tree branch twirling around it like she was performing at the Olympics and stopped, hanging still from the branch staring at me with a competitive smile.

Arashi let go of the branch and fell straight down landing on her feet. We walked towards each other slowly, both grinning and ready for the unexpected. When we made it back in the clearing, we went back into stance this time switching to a boxing stance. Arashi gave a quick jab, as I blocked and turned to give her an elbow to the stomach.

Arashi immediately countered by giving me a blow to the ribs. We went back and forth with blows to the face; chest and stomach like were fighting for the belt. I jumped in the air flipping backwards landing down in a crouch sending two blades directly at Arashi. She deflected them using the bands she wore around her wrists that can easy be mistaken as accessories.

She ran towards me in full speed blinking in and out as I prepared myself for her attack. She tackled me causing us to crash onto the ground leaving a deep line in the surface behind us. I gripped on to Arashi waiting until the last minute throwing her over my head sending her crashing into a tree.

I waited for Arashi to get up and come back through the trees but suddenly I was hit from behind taking the same flight through the trees as Arashi. I got up leaping through the trees making noise so that Arashi can know exactly where I was. She followed my noise leaping from tree to tree.

I laughed taunting her as I jumped blinking in and out of sight until I blinked in front of Arashi knocking her out the trees. Arashi, although surprised landed on her feet and looked up at me as I returned back to the ground. We were about to go another round until Bruce stopped us 'saying that's enough girls'. Arashi and I stopped and started laughing and playing about who got who.

"As weird as that was to watch I think it will be better for you two to train with separate partners." Bruce said confused at how we can go back to normal after such an intense practice.

"That's fine we just wanted to demonstrate how we practice to get started." I said responding to Bruce.

"Yea we just have fun with it." Arashi said making funny gestures at Bruce.

"Well I will hate to see you two in a real battle against each other." Bruce said shaking his head.

"It wasn't that bad." I said.

"If you really wanted some action you should have lets us keep going." Arashi said patting Bruce on the shoulder.

"I won't attack my brother full on like that?" Nathaniel said with concern in his voice for what he might do to Joel."

"That's why you won't be training with your brother. You want to protect him from harm which will make it hard for you to push him to his limits." I said hoping Nathaniel could see we only wanted to get Joel to really know his strengths.

"I understand why I just need to process it more." Nathaniel said.

"Why are you worried anyway? He's training with Dante? There equal in strength and speed." Arashi said making her way over to Joel.

"That's not why I'm worried. I want Joel to be at his best. I just have to accept that the way to get him there is for him to train with one of us." Nathaniel said with a panicked look on his face as he creates flashes in his head of hurting his own brother.

"Nathaniel I will be perfectly fine. Time to let me grow up." Joel said walking over to Nathaniel and resting his hand on his shoulder to confirm he's ready.

"Good. You and Dante need to take it slow the first round so that you can get a feel of each other strengths." Bruce said noticing the tension between Dante and Joel.

They both nodded and went to take their positions across from each other on the so called battle field we created.

Joel had a warriors stance looking as if he has years of battles under his belt way beyond his age. Dante had the basic kung Fu stance taught to us by sensei Arobi. The intensity in the air was almost unbearable. We could feel the dislike between the two and felt like the fires of hell was about to wash over us. We watched as they stayed locked in their positions staring at one another as if waiting for the other to strike. I glanced over at Nathaniel whose face was bald up impatient to see what Joel can do. I returned my attention back to Joel and Dante as Dante went to strike first getting knocked down by a blocking kick from Joel.

Joel stayed in that position with his leg still in the air giving Dante a fierce look. As Dante got up Joel slowly lowered his leg back down facing Dante head on. It was almost as if he was Ryu from street fighter fighting cane from mortal combat.

I couldn't believe how well Joel fights giving how over

protective Nathaniel is over him. I couldn't help but wonder just how strong Nathaniel is. Dante looked as if he was focused now, being that he underestimated his opponent. Joel made the first move now charging towards Dante with given intentions on how he will strike.

When he made it close to Dante his arm went back to give a full force punch missing Dante by a hair as he moved out the way giving Joel a low kick in the stomach. Joel moved back barely an inch from the blow. He looked up at Dante from a crouched position and retuned a full blow to Dante's stomach sending him crashing into a tree trunk.

We can all see how mad Dante is getting. He used his anger while fighting instead of paying attention to Joel techniques. The fight got even more intense as they went at each other no longer blocking blows. It didn't change the fact that Joel was wiping the floor with Dante.

I put my attention back on Nathaniel as his face was still serious but showed how proud he was of Joel. Arashi made it noticeable exactly who she was cheering for. Every time Joel will hit Dante Arashi will make different comments cheering him on. Bruce facial expression was the same as mine.

We both were surprised and clearly underestimated Joel ourselves. Bruce stopped the fight seeing that Dante was out of his element. He has a lot to learn with not enough time to learn it. Dante didn't want to stop. He still felt like he had a chance but Joel ended it with a blow to his chest sending him flying. Dante landed on the ground gripping his chest from the pain caused by Joel's blow. Bruce went to check on Dante as Arashi ran to Joel jumping in his arms. Nathaniel and I stayed glued to our spots, me with a look of confusion on my face and Nathaniel looking like a proud parent.

"That's enough for now." Bruce said taking Dante into the house.

"That was very impressive Joel." I said still a little caught off guard.

"Yes. Well done." Nathaniel said giving Joel praise.

"Thank you." Joel said slipping right back into his modest attitude.

"I already knew you were going to win." Arashi said still holding on to Joel.

Joel smiled as him and Arashi headed back into the house laughing and joking around with each other no longer hiding their attraction to each other. I started to go in the house to check on Dante but I was stopped by Nathaniel grabbing my hand.

"I want to thank you for getting my birth certificate." Nathaniel said with sincerity in his eyes.

"There's no need to thank me I wanted to help." I said placing my hand on his shoulder.

"Thank you." Nathaniel said holding my gaze.

I smiled back at Nathaniel removing my hand and turned to head back in the house. When I entered Arashi and Joel were sitting on the couch still caught up in each other's company. Bruce was still looking over Dante even though he was completely healed. I took a seat on the couch waiting to see what Bruce has come up with. I can tell by the look on Dante's face that this was not over between him and Joel. He wanted a rematch bad only he didn't want it during training.

Joel was too caught up in Arashi to notice Dante's glare at him. This has been the first time I can honestly see how at peace Joel is when he's with Arashi. Arashi never showed much interest in any male before like she has with Joel. This is something new for the both of them. They are extremely attracted to each other and I think it has more to do with who we are that increases their feelings for one another.

My attention was drawn away from them when Bruce came over and had a seat after his examination of Dante.

"That is some skill you have their Joel." Bruce said.

"Thank you sir." Joel responded.

"You and your brother must train harder than you give yourselves credit for." Bruce said moving his attention to Nathaniel.

"No. I never harm Joel when we are training." Nathaniel said noticing the confusion on Bruce face.

"Where did you learn your control if not from your brother?" Bruce asked Joel.

"Our sensei knew that Nathaniel will never do anything to harm me even if it meant preparing me for the worst so he trained me how to reach my full potential in separate trainings when he sent Nathaniel out for days at a time." Joel said looking at Nathaniel.

"Why didn't you tell me?" Nathaniel asked.

"Would it really have changed anything?" Joel asked Nathaniel.

"I don't know." Nathaniel said looking away from Joel.

"I just wanted you to be proud of me without having to worry so much about me. I didn't think we will ever be in the mess were in now." Joel said explaining himself to Nathaniel.

"It's ok. I understand and I am extremely proud of you." Nathaniel said smiling at Joel.

Joel face lit up as he went to hug Nathaniel.

Afterword's Joel and Arashi went back to being mushy.

"So what do we do now Bruce?" I asked.

"You four will train together and I will train Dante myself." Bruce said still watching Joel. He couldn't believe how much he over powered Dante seeing that they should be of equal strength.

"We need to eat something first I'm starving." Arashi said heading to the kitchen.

"Does she ever stop eating?" Bruce asked going behind Arashi to make sure she doesn't eat all the food.

I laughed and went up to my room. I was hungry but I wanted to relax a little. So I laid back on my bed and closed my eyes for a minute. It felt good to be able to get some peace and quiet without having to worry about anything. I cleared my head and relaxed my body as I drifted slowly to sleep.

I jumped up feeling another presence near me. It was Nathaniel standing at the edge of the bed with a sad look on his face holding his papers. I got up waiting for him to say something but all he did was stand there gripping the papers in his hand into a ball.

"What's going on?" I asked wanting to know why he is so intense and in my room. Nathaniel didn't say anything just handed me the papers. I opened them noticing that one is his birth certificate, another one Joel's and the last one his birth mother's. The birth certificates were normal except Joel's. It was a copy that listed a different name on it under mother's name that was not on Nathaniel's. I looked up at Nathaniel who was getting madder by the second so I went to him giving him a huge hug.

"It's okay. We will figure it out. I'm sure it's just Seth trying to pull your strings. This isn't even a real birth certificate. He could have made this his self. Don't worry. I promise we will get to the bottom of this together. Ok?" I said lifting his head so that I can look in his eyes to ensure him that we will find out what's going on.

"I don't want him to see this. Can you keep this safe for me?" Nathaniel asked.

"Of course." I said going to a hidden opening in the floor and placing it there.

"Thank you." Nathaniel said and left my room.

I waited a minute before I headed back down stairs to join the others. I shook off my tiredness then went to join the others. I made it downstairs and noticed that not much have changed. Arashi and Joel was still hugged up, Dante was outside training alone still heated from his defeat from Joel, Bruce was in the kitchen getting dinner started and Nathaniel was standing in the door watching Dante train.

I walked in the kitchen to see what Bruce was cooking up. Whatever it was smelled great.

"What you cooking in here Bruce." I asked wanting to look in the oven and see what it was.

"Roast with potatoes, carrots, green peppers and onions. With some homemade garlic bread and salad." Bruce said taking in the smell of the aromas.

"Sounds delicious I can't wait." I said going into the cabinet to grab some chips to hold me over until the food is ready.

I walked over to the door beside Nathaniel to see how Dante was doing with his training.

"He has very little training. Did he not have a sensei?" Nathaniel asked.

"He started off training with me and Arashi until his father came and took him away. He was very young at the time and Arobi really didn't get the chance to train him." I said watching Dante. I noticed what areas he needed the most help in.

"How is he going to learn in such a short time?"

Nathaniel asked.

"Bruce may not look like much but he can bring the best out of Dante." I said.

"I'm not second guessing Bruce. It's Dante he's not willing to accept help." Nathaniel said.

"Well let's see." I said as I walked out to join Dante.

"Do you mind if I join you?" I asked Dante as I walked up to him.

"You don't have to baby me. I can handle myself." Dante said as he continued to strike the air.

"I know. I just want to spar with you so you can stop attacking the air." I said waiting for him to accept my invitation.

"Okay but don't treat me like I can't handle myself." Dante said as I walked up to him.

"I won't. I love a challenge just as much as you do." I said.

Dante attacked me trying to catch me off guard but I countered by grabbing him and slamming him into the ground. I didn't have to be so rough but I wanted him to see I wasn't going to go easy on him. He got up angry coming at me so unfocused and unbalanced that it didn't take much but a nudge to knock him down again.

"You're not focused. Let go of your anger and pay attention." I said to Dante as he got up and whipped himself up angrier than before.

Dante attacked again still angry. I was able to trick him into following me in the air just to kick him back down. I landed on top off him using my foot to hold him down. He struggled trying to get me off him but was not able to get me to budge. I can see him starting to get more angry and losing focus.

"Stop trying to get me off you and let go of your anger and focus on how to get me off you." I said trying to get Dante to focus.

I saw him as he relaxed and let go of his anger enough to grab my foot and twist it causing me to fall off him. I could have flipped and landed on my feet but I wanted him to see what he can do if he just focused. I rolled on the ground getting up several feet away from him smiling, happy to see him taking in what I told him. By now everyone has step outside to watch us spar. I was glad to see Dante more focused on his attacks than the watching eyes of our audience.

I charged towards him making my next move obvious to see if he will notice. I jumped into a spinning kick allowing Dante to catch me and toss me away. This time instead of rolling over I landed on my feet coming right back for him at a faster pace.

I stopped directly in front of him giving him hit after hit making my hits stronger and stronger. Dante noticed and broke free. Using our surrounding to get me to come after him, I followed him as he leaped in and out of trees vanishing in and out. I could catch him if I wanted to but I had something else up my sleeve.

I blinked out reappearing in front of him knocking him out the trees. Dante paid attention using gravity as a friend instead of an enemy flipping and landing in a crouch. I landed in front of him with a smile of praise on my face.

"Good job. You learn fast." I said to Dante giving him a compliment.

"Thank you for not going easy on me." Dante said in return.

"No problem." I said giving a small nod.

"Dinner is ready." Bruce called out to us.

"Wow, how time has flown." I said surprised at how fast the day went past.

We all went into the kitchen rushing to sit so we can eat. We all shared at least one thing in common and that is the love of food. We passed the food around making our plates and eating in silence. We were hungry before but now it's like we haven't ate in months. We looked like savages torturing our meal. After we were done eating we called it a night escaping to our rooms ending yet another night.

Chapter Seven

I was woken by the sun shining in my window. I didn't open my eyes. I just laid there like I do every morning. I could hear Arashi thoughts but I ignored them pretending like I'm sleep.

"Adena I know you're not sleep I can hear your thoughts." Arashi said irritated that I will try to play sleep.

"What do you want Arashi?" I asked still not opening my eyes.

"For you to get your ass up." Arashi snapped back.

"Why should I?" I asked.

"I need to talk to you about Joel." Arashi said surprising me. I opened my eyes immediately sitting up to face Arashi. I wanted to touch her forehead to see if she was ok but we never get sick. This was new. Arashi

never needed to talk about a guy she was sleeping with.
"What's going on?" I said not knowing what to expect.
Arashi was blocking her thoughts from me so I had to
wait for her to tell me.

"Something's not right about him and Nathaniel."
Arashi said looking at me waiting for my reaction. I
just sat there with no reaction waiting for her to tell me
why she felt that way.

"Ok why do you think that?" I asked not knowing why
I had to.

"You saw him fight Dante yesterday. Even if he is
more trained then Dante there's no way he should
have over powered him like that. Even Nathaniel was
surprised. He is almost as strong as we are. I can even
tell when we're having sex by how he handles me and
he wouldn't be able to overpower me if his strength
was the same as Dante's." Arashi said sitting down
next to me showing a side of her I never seen before.
She really cares for Joel but feels like something is
wrong about him.

"Well there's only one way to find out." I said to
Arashi putting my serious face on.

"What?" Arashi said looking at me anxiously in the eyes.

"You have to sleep with Dante." I said falling out into a non-stopping laugh.

"Adena I'm serious." Arashi said not finding my joke funny.

"I know. I guess it has something to do with what Nathaniel showed me yesterday." I said walking over to where I put Nathaniel papers.

"Showed you?" Arashi said going back into her regular self.

"Get your head out the gutter. Their birth certificates are completely different." I said as I handed them over to Arashi. She took a minute to look them over.

"According to these they're not brothers." Arashi said looking at me.

"I know. Nathaniel thinks it's another scam Seth was using to get to him."

"How can he know that for sure?"

"I don't know. I told him we will do everything we can to find out."

"Well they both need to be prepared for this if it's

fake." Arashi said getting up.

"You can't tell Joel. I promised Nathaniel I will keep it from him until we figure it out." I told Arashi.

"He needs to know." Arashi said.

"I know you have feelings for Joel but how do you know he doesn't already know. Let him come to you but don't tell him about this until we figure it out. Nathaniel should be the one to tell him not you or me." I said hoping Arashi don't let her feelings for Joel get to her.

"Ok I won't." Arashi said leaving my room.

I put Nathaniel papers back in the floor. I wasn't tired anymore so I got in the shower and got dressed. As usual when I went downstairs Bruce was in the kitchen making breakfast. I went to the refrigerator to get some juice then headed outside for some air. It felt nice today, the sky is clear and the sun is shining. I climbed one of the tall trees to sit at the very top on a branch so that I can see the view. It is beautiful. I'm interrupted when Bruce came out calling my name since he didn't see where I went. I jumped down landing in front of him.

"What was you doing up there?" Bruce asked.

"Nothing just enjoying the view." I answered.

"Oh ok. Breakfast is ready." Bruce said walking back inside.

I went inside and set at the table. Everyone was already at the table besides Arashi. Arashi came down the stairs with my phone as it was ringing.

"It's Quentin Adena." Arashi said as she brought me my phone. I got up and met her so I can step away to answer.

"Hello." I said walking towards the stairs to take the call to my room.

"You know you should be more careful about who you're affectionate with in public." A voice other than Quentin said. I froze in spot looking at my phone to make sure it was the right number and it was. The name on my caller id says Quentin.

"Who is this?" I asked as I felt Arashi come to stand by my side.

"Aw don't tell me you forgot about me already. I thought we had a connection or did Nathaniel beat me to the pot?" The man said on the phone. I immediately knew who it was.

"Seth." I said furious already knowing he done something to Quentin.

"Yes. I knew we had something." Seth said with taunting satisfaction in his voice.

"Where is Quentin?" I asked tired of his game.

"Depends on what I get for telling you." Seth responded.

"Your head on a platter." I said visioning it in my head.

"Let's not get nasty if you want to see your boyfriend again." Seth said.

"What do you want?" I asked.

"You took my pet away and I need another. So I thought to myself why not you." Seth said with a deceitful laugh.

I can feel myself changing. I was getting angrier and angrier. I dropped the phone standing in place only concentrating on Seth's voice. I saw Arashi pick up the phone but I had no idea what she was saying. I was so far gone in anger I blocked my surroundings out. The only thing I was worried about was getting Quentin back. Arashi stepped in front of me with Nathaniel by her side. Both trying to get through to me but I can no longer hear them. Everything went red and I knew my eyes had change.

"Adena calm down. We will get him back." Arashi was yelling.

"Adena you have to calm down." Nathaniel said.

"Guys I think it's too late. You better step back." Bruce yelled out.

"Adena think about it he wants you to get mad. Calm down." Arashi said.

It was already too late. I blinked out reappearing in Quentin's place. I looked around for a minute trying to see if something was left behind. Quentin's place was untouched which means Seth grabbed him from the club. Without hesitation I appeared at the club standing by the bar. I heard security scream out to me wandering how I got in.

"Hey how did you get in here?" Security said. I continued to walk and look around but nothing was out the ordinary.

"Stop right there lady. That's the last time I'm going to

say it." The security guard said waiting a few seconds for me to respond. When I didn't he came behind me gripping my arm. I turned around to face him and saw the scared look on his face when he saw my eyes. His hands gripped harder around my arm so I grabbed his shoulder squeezing it than throwing him across the room.

"Adena is that you?" He said recognizing me. I didn't answer. I walked to the back of the club and exited into the alley. There were tire marks on the ground. This is where they grabbed him. I followed the tire marks every which way they went disrupting traffic and damaging cars on the way. There were a lot of people blowing their horns and yelling that instantly stopped when they caught the look in my eyes. No one knew what was going on but they wasn't about to find out the hard way.

I finally made it to the where the tracks ended and it was in a building garage on the top floor not far from where Nathaniel lives. They had to get rid of the car here and either went on foot or in another car. I listen to the sounds and voices around me for Seth or

Quentin's voice. Things were quiet besides the usual busy streets. Then I heard Seth's voice. *"Let's get out of here."* Seth said.

I concentrated on his voice and with a blink of an eye I was standing in front of Seth. I'm angry and my eyes are fuming red. Seth is caught by surprise. He froze staring into my eyes. The other guy with him attempted to attack me from behind. I turned giving a blow to the chest killing him instantly. I turned back to Seth as he tried to run and sent him flying across the room.

"Where is Quentin?" I asked filled with anger.

"You will never know if you kill me." Seth said using another diversion to try and say his own life.

I lifted him up by his head holding him in the air. I felt something come over me like a cool rush going through my body. Before I knew it I was seeing and hearing every memory or thought Seth had ever had. I snapped out of it releasing his head and grabbing his neck.

"You gave him to Rin?" I snapped as I pinned him to the wall.

"Yes. When I saw you two being intimate in the club I figured what better way to get my bounty." Seth said with a grin on his face.

"All you did was ensure both your deaths." I said as I squeezed his neck.

I have all intentions of killing him slowly, watching him struggle for air as his breath leaves his body. The sight of him slowly dying brings a satisfying smile to my face. At this moment in time nothing feels better than the power I have over him. I watched as the smile he just had disappeared and fade into need. I watched as in his last moment instead of him accepting his death he still fought to live. He wasn't expecting for his plan to back fire and land in his lap. I dropped him like a kid wanting a better toy and headed out the door. I tried concentrating on Quentin so that I can go straight to him but all my attempts were block by Arashi. She was not by my side but a nagging voice in my head.

"Adena stop you need to calm down so you can think things through."

"I'm done waiting now get out of my head."

"This is exactly what they want. You're walking straight into a trap."

"No, I'm eliminating the problem."

"You're putting Quentin in more danger. They will kill him on the spot as soon as they see you and in the end they still would have won. Let me help you. We do this together like we always have."

Arashi stayed quiet as I thought things through. I was still furious but I did understand that I was putting Quentin in more danger. I focused on Quentin face and the disappointment on Arashi face as I started to calm down and return to myself. I saw everything clearer now, I feel like I just shook off a wave of pure evil. I am weak, tired from holding so much rage for so long I'm wearing myself out. I thought about Arashi and was suddenly back at the safe house. Arashi walked up to me asking me if I was alright but all I can do was look at her before I collapsed hitting the floor. Everything went black and I slipped deeper and deeper into the darkness and then I was out.

I woke up a little dizzy so I laid there for a minute. When my vision came back I noticed I was in my room. My blinds were closed blocking my view outside. I felt alone. I tried to get up and open the blinds but I was still a little dizzy. I laid there and closed my eyes relaxing and trying not to push myself up. I cleared my head of all thoughts and just laid there in peace. It was quiet for a minute and then I heard the others talking.

"I'm going to check on her." Arashi said.

"Just leave her be. She will come down when she's ready." Bruce said.

"This has never happened before. We don't even get sick." Arashi said.

"She was really gone when she got angry. It took a lot of energy from her to hold all that hate." Joel said.

"She's getting stronger but it's draining her." Bruce said.

"It's not a weakness. Adena has always had an attitude problem. It's always been easy to piss her off but she controls it well." Arashi said.

"It's different when the one's you love are involved. How will you react if someone told you they had Adena hostage?" Nathaniel said.

"I will laugh. It's impossible for someone to keep her hostage.

Did you not see her go crazy?" Arashi said.

"He's just saying..." Dante started to say before interrupted by Arashi.

"I know what he's saying. I would have been just as mad."
Arashi said.

"She will be fine. She's a strong person." Bruce said.

Everyone was quiet now. Moving back and forth waiting for what state of mind I will be in when I get up. I didn't want them to worry but I'm still set on going and getting Quentin. There is no way I'm just leaving him there. Rin knows we're coming for him so the best way is to give him something he's not expecting. A clear knock on his door.

It was time to face the crowd so I got up and headed down stairs. Everyone is pretty much lounging around. I took the final step down and everyone turned and looked at me without saying a word. I looked at them individually waiting for someone to speak but they were frozen in silence.

"It's ok I'm not going to go crazy and kill you all." I said walking over to the kitchen to get something to drink.

"We just want to make sure you ok and not crowd you." Nathaniel said.

"I'm fine." I said as I turned to be tackled by Arashi with hugs and threats.

"Do you know how crazy you went? It was exciting to see you let loose a little." Arashi said laughing at my loss of control.

"Arashi!" Bruce said.

"I'm just saying besides the whole going evil on us thing, you kick ass." Arashi said.

"Thank you I think." I said back to Arashi.

"I know you still want to go and get Quentin but I think its best we work on our plan." Nathaniel said.

"I have a plan." I said looking at Nathaniel.

"What is it?" Dante asked.

"Walk right up to the door and knock." I said.

"You're joking right?" Nathaniel said.

"Not at all." I said.

"You will be risking your life and Quentin's if you do that." Nathaniel said.

"Quentin will be fine." I said turning to get some snacks out the kitchen cabinet.

"Arashi you need to talk to Adena." Joel said.

"She's right. It's the best way to throw him off." Arashi said.

"What?" Joel said confused by Arashi decision.

"I can't explain it but I understand what Adena is talking about. It's a good idea. You just have to trust me." Arashi said looking into Joel's eyes.

Joel frowned. He was not in complete agreement with the plan but he didn't want to fight Arashi on it in front of me. Arashi knows what my plan is but also knows I'm still pissed I put Quentin in the middle of our problem.

I walked outside and started to do some light training to channel my anger. I want to be able to tap into my anger without draining myself. I tried a number of ways to get myself angry enough to channel my abilities but nothing worked.

"You want some help?" Nathaniel said coming outside after watching my attempts fail.

"Not if you're going to hold back." I said moving on to try something else.

"I won't." Nathaniel said.

"This should be interesting." I said walking towards Nathaniel.

Nathaniel just gave me a firm look as we started walking in circles waiting for one or the other to make a move. I'm usually not the first to attack but we are running out of time. I attacked with full strength giving Nathaniel a blow to the stomach.

My blow only made him step back like an adult playing a role with his child. So I attacked again this time jumping on his shoulders rapping my legs around his neck to flip him but he gripped his hands on my thighs stopping me from moving. I don't understand how he is so much stronger than me. So I put the heels of my foot into his back pulling myself closer and closer to him, choking him with my legs.

That's when I noticed the slight change in his eyes. They were mixed hazel brown with grey in them. Nathaniel noticed me staring at his eyes and undoes my grip throwing me off him on the ground. I could have gotten right up but I was shocked by his ability to control himself.

"You taped into your abilities. How?" I asked getting

up off the ground.

"Your abilities are tied to your emotions. Tap into it that way." Nathaniel said as he walked towards me.

"I have been. It's not working for me." I said watching his every move.

"No you haven't. You were trying to tap into your anger which you have no control over." Nathaniel said now standing right in front of me.

He made me feel uneasy. I wasn't scared of him but I was curious of just how strong he can get. The look in his eyes was neither good nor evil but it felt unsafe. I stood there ready for anything as Nathaniel looked deep into my eyes.

I could tell he didn't want to hurt me but he didn't want anyone else to either. I watched as he snapped out of it and came to, giving me a blow that sent me flying across the forest. I turned landing on my feet crouched over accessing over Nathaniel, trying to figure out what's his next move. I stood up when Nathaniel was suddenly standing in front of me again. This time with pain in his eyes. Nathaniel eyes were back to normal and I used it as an advantage and hit him with a blow to the chest sending him flying towards the house. I watched as he kept his eyes on me until the last moment before flipping and landing on his feet capturing my eyes again.

"That's enough for now." Nathaniel said as he turned to go back into the house.

"Wait." I said stopping Nathaniel. He turned and looked at me with hurt in his eyes so instead of holding him there I let him go.

"Never mind." I said.

"Is everything ok?" Arashi said walking outside bypassing Nathaniel.

"Fine." I said to Arashi. *"I need you to get everyone out the house so I can talk to Nathaniel."* I thought to Arashi as she walked back in the house.

"Why what's going on?" Arashi asked.

"Something's wrong with Nathaniel and I need to see what it is but I got a feeling he won't tell me if everyone is here."

"Ok I'll see what I can do." Arashi said.

"Thank you." I responded.

Arashi went in the kitchen writing things down that we may or may not need at the moment. One list was for kitchen things and the other was equipment and weapons for training. When she was done she gathered Bruce, Dante and Joel asking them to join her to get the things off her list. They were ready to get out the house anyway and agreed to go.

"Adena we're going out for a couple of things do you want to come?" Arashi asked me.

"No I think I'll pass this time." I said.

"Ok. Do you want something back?" Arashi said playing it off well.

"Some snacks please." I said grinning at Arashi as she rolled her eyes.

"Ok. Be back soon." Arashi said walking out the door. I grabbed some snacks and something to drink and then headed to my room. I want to talk to Nathaniel but I have a craving for sweets after our training. I headed to my room opening my pop taking a drink as I entered my room. When I moved the bottle from my mouth I saw Nathaniel sitting on my bed.

"How long have you been in here?" I asked surprised once again by him being in my room.

"I wanted to talk to you. Is it ok?" Nathaniel asked.

"Yea what's up?" I said still standing at the door.

"I'm sorry do you want me to get up so you can have your bed." Nathaniel said quickly getting up.

"No it's fine. Have a seat." I said and walked to the other end of the bed and sat down.

"It's about Joel. Something's not right. Even with our training he still should not be that strong." Nathaniel started to say.

"I know. Nathaniel there's something I need to tell you about when I went after Seth." I said avoiding eye contact.

"What is it?" Nathaniel asked.

"Before I killed Seth I asked him to tell me where Quentin is. He refused so I put my hands on his head to slowly squeeze it before killing him but instead a rush of power came over me and suddenly I was seeing and hearing every thought he has ever had. The birth certificate's he gave you is real and there's much more to go with it. Nathaniel, Joel is not your brother."

"Then who is he?" Nathaniel asked not really surprised by the information but disappointed.

"It doesn't bother you?" I asked confused by his reaction.

"I feared it would be something like that so I prepared myself for the worst." Nathaniel said.

"I'm sorry." I said voicing my sympathy.

"I'm fine. No matter what happens he will still be my brother." Nathaniel said.

"Well you're not going to like what I have to tell you next." I said catching his attention once more.

"What is it?" Nathaniel asked.

"You really do have a brother out there. His name is Thaddeus and he was switched with Joel at birth." I said pausing to see how Nathaniel will take the news.

"What? What are you saying?" Nathaniel said standing up.

"Your mother hid Thaddeus and took you to father Reed so that he can give you to Sensei Gin to raise and train you when she learned you may grow up with abilities. Father Reed died that same year leaving you and another little boy like you behind. That little boy was Joel. When you were found Joel was still a baby and you were a toddler. Everyone just assumed you were brothers.

Seth knew all about you then and went looking for you at different orphanages and churches. You and Joel were long gone by the time he made it to Father Reed's church. He searched through all of Father Reeds papers and found both of your birth certificates. He tracked your mother down. When she didn't tell him where you were he killed her. The same with Joel's mother.

Thaddeus is still out there somewhere not knowing who he really is. Seth was using you to find and kill him and then planned on killing you too until the bounty on Arashi and I came to part. When he found out that there are more like you he used you using those papers to control you. He never planned on giving them to you. He figured you were going to die by him or us anyway." I explained as Nathaniel sat back down processing the information.

"I have a brother out there." Nathaniel said to himself.

"Yes and I think it's time you find him before someone else does." I told Nathaniel.

"Yea." Nathaniel said still processing.

"What are you going to tell Joel?" I asked Nathaniel.

"Nothing right now. I'll tell him when we get Quentin back." Nathaniel said as his focus came back to me.

"I understand that your brother is your first priority. You don't have to help me get Quentin back." I said surprised that he would still help me when he should be looking for his brother.

"I want to. Besides you're doing the same for me." Nathaniel said.

"I am willing to help if you want me to." I said.

"You already have. Thank you." Nathaniel said smiling at me as I blushed trying to hide my feelings.

"The others should be back soon." I said changing the subject.

"Well we should train and get you ready while we have some time alone." Nathaniel said.

"I'll like that." I said leading the way out my room.

Chapter Eight

Nathaniel and I finished training as the others returned back from there outing. I finally learned how to channel my emotion and tie it in with my abilities. I was ready, now it's time for me and Nathaniel to get the other's ready.

We decided to keep the information about Joel and Thaddeus a secret until we got Quentin back. I don't understand why Nathaniel wants to help me get the man I love back rather than start the search for his brother.

"All hot and bothered. What were you two doing while we were gone?" Arashi asked accusing us of having sex.

"We were only training. Get your head out the gutter Arashi." I said.

"Nathaniel did you give Adena a good time?" Arashi asked Nathaniel receiving a surprised glare from me.

"It is as she says. We just trained." Nathaniel responded laughing at my reaction.

"Too bad." Arashi said.

"Anyway you guys need to start training. The sooner we leave the better." I said walking past everyone heading upstairs to my room to take a shower.

"We need a plan b Adena. Just in case knocking on the door won't work." Dante said.

"I got it covered just make sure you're ready." I said.

"What does that mean? You want us to hide in the bushes and wait for a signal to jump out?" Dante asked showing how irritated he is with the lack of information.

"I will explain later." I said as I went to my room to clean myself up.

The warm water from the shower felt so good against my skin. I washed myself over and over thinking it would solve all our problems, but it did nothing to remove the hurt I felt for getting Quentin involved in this. If I wouldn't have sent the package to his club, they wouldn't have known about Quentin. The thought just kept playing over and over in my head until tears started to pour down my cheeks. I held back a sob and let the water from the shower run over my face to hide my tears. I have no idea why when I'm alone in the shower. I must have lost myself in my emotions because I didn't notice that someone was in the bathroom with me until I heard his voice.

"Adena, are you okay?" Nathaniel asked from outside the shower.

"Nathaniel! What the hell are you doing in my bathroom?" I said really feeling like he overstepped the boundaries.

"I came to check on you and I heard you crying." Nathaniel said with concern in his voice.

I didn't notice that I was crying out loud. I thought I was controlling my sobs and washing them away in the water.

"I'm fine Nathaniel, thank you for checking up on me." I said still feeling a little weird about him being in the bathroom with me while I'm in the shower. I'm crying over Quentin but at the same time wanting

Nathaniel to take my mind off the hurt.

"Okay. I'll leave you alone then." Nathaniel said slowly taking his exit.

"Nathaniel." I called to him in yearning not wanting him to leave me alone, but not wanting him to stay either because I knew I might not be able to push him away this time.

"Yes Adena." He said coming to stand closer to the shower than before. I can see his shadow through my shower curtain.

"Nothing." I said once again running from the feelings I have for Nathaniel.

Nathaniel didn't move from the spot he stood in for what felt like a long minute. When he did I had the urge to get out the shower and go after him. Instead, when he moved away I took a deep breath and reached for the curtain. I stopped myself and dropped my hand back down to let him go. I was confused. I didn't want him to go. But I couldn't stop thinking about Quentin either. The next thing I knew the shower curtain slid open and Nathaniel stepped into the shower with me.

"Nathaniel….." I said his name wanting to ask him what he was doing before he cut me off.

"Shhhh." He said wrapping his arms around me. "Just let me hold you." Nathaniel said with love in his eyes. I wanted to protest and tell him to get out but my body yielded to him, giving in to what I really wanted. I laid my head on his chest and continued my low sobbing as Nathaniel held on to me and pulled us both under the water. He repeated over and over to me everything will be okay and in that moment I believed him and tried to relax.

Nathaniel is being careful with me not wanting to break the connection we have now so he said nothing to me as he picked up my body wash and poured some on my shower sponge. He stood there looking at me with the sponge held up asking me for permission to wash me. I nodded my approval and he begin washing my body while at the same time not looking away from me. He held my gaze to his as I relaxed under his touch. He washed me with slow circular motions starting from my neck and working his way slowly down to my breast. He reached my breast and never took his eyes off me as he washed one breast with the shower sponge and caressed the other breast with his hand.

His touch got more intense squeezing my breast and pulling my nipples. After he washed, teased and caressed my breast, he started his slow circular movement again down my stomach. I noticed where he was working his way to and I wanted him there so bad.

I closed my eyes and tilted my head back waiting for him to make it down to my pussy. I was suddenly aroused and excited. I noticed he had dropped the shower sponge and his open hand was now moving slowly down my stomach until he reached my pussy. He used his middle finger to push into my folds and caress my clit. I couldn't help the moan that escaped from me. He applied pressure to my clit making me react by pushing back against him and squirming to the feeling. He wrapped his other arm around my waist to hold me in place while he started aggressively caressing my clit faster and faster, holding me in place so that I have to take every single pleasure going into my body.

I gripped my hands behind his neck and exploded, Cumming in his hand. I called out his name but he wasn't through with me. He kept going with his tortuous assault on my clit making me build up again and fight against him trying to run from the overwhelming feeling coming over me again. "Nathaniel." I said trying to plead with him but he kept going harder, faster, harder, faster until I exploded again convulsing over and over as he held me in his unbreakable grip before finally falling back into him. He held me for a minute allowing me to regain my balance before he finished washing me.

I could do nothing but let him as I tried to control the shivers that were going through my body. When Nathaniel finished he shut off the water and wrapped me in my towel I had thrown over the shower rod. He stepped out the shower onto the carpet on the floor and dried his feet.

He picked me up, carrying me out the shower and took me back in my room to lay me in my bed. I watched him as he lifted my blanket so that I can scoot under it. I couldn't take my eyes off his naked body. He was very fit and sexy as hell. I looked up and down his body over and over before finally making eye contact with him when he scooted in next to me and pulled me close to him.

"Sleep now." Nathaniel said to me as I watched him carefully. I silently listened to him and drifted off to sleep.

I woke up feeling better and turned around to thank Nathaniel but he was already gone. I got up and noticed it was dark outside so I looked at my clock and it was 3:17 in the morning. I took the towel off me that I was still wrapped in and put on my robe. I went downstairs to get something to drink and Nathaniel was sitting on the couch drinking a glass of water. He turned and looked at me when he noticed I was standing at the end of the stairs watching him. I finally walked down the final stair and spoke.

"You're up early" I said trying to break the ice.

"So are you. You need your rest Adena. You should go back to bed." Nathaniel said with an intense look on his face.

"I feel fine Nathaniel. You weren't there when I woke up. Is everything ok?" I asked trying to figure out why he was in a sober mood.

Nathaniel looked at me and walked over to stand right in front of me before he spoke.

"I'm fine. I didn't think you will notice I was gone." Nathaniel said waiting for my reaction.

"I wanted to thank you for taking care of me but when I turned around you were gone." I said trying to hold my composure. I didn't want him to see how much he affected me, but the longer I stood this close to him, the more my body wanted him. It was as if he already knew that and closed the space between us even more making me hold my breath to stop from jumping in his arms.

"Oh. You're welcome. It's my pleasure to assist in any way I can." Nathaniel said looking down at me with passion in his eyes.

I stood there for a minute while he held my gaze before I broke the connection and walked to the kitchen to get some juice. I poured a glass and drunk it straight down and then poured myself another one.

Something is up with Nathaniel but he's distracting me the one way he knows how. He knows I can't handle how I feel about him when he's that close to me.

"Nathaniel you know you can talk to me if you have something on your mind." I said.

"Really." Nathaniel said walking towards me.

"You don't need to distract me." I said walking away from him, mad that he's trying to distract me again. "If you don't want to tell me what's bothering you then just say you don't want to talk." I said with more attitude then I expected.

Nathaniel stopped in his tracks with a confused look on his face. He opened his mouth to say something and then closed it back.

"What?" I said wondering what was on his mind.

"I'm not trying to distract you and it's not that I don't want to talk. I........I just" Nathaniel was about to say something else until he was interrupted by Bruce coming down the stairs.

"What are you two doing up so early? It's too early to be training." Bruce said wondering why we're standing in the dark looking at each other.

Nathaniel walked away and went back upstairs. I'm assuming he's going back to his room. I looked at Bruce and gave him a shy smile.

"We both couldn't sleep and ended up down here for something to drink. Me shortly after him." I said trying to clarify.

"Okay." Bruce said with a kind smile on his face.

"What are you doing up so early Bruce?" I asked curious.

"An old man like me don't sleep that long anymore. I enjoy the peace I have at this hour." Bruce said looking outside into the forest.

"Yes it is peaceful at this hour." I said understanding how he felt.

I left Bruce to enjoy his peace as I sat on the couch to finish my juice. My mind drifted off as I sat back and closed my eyes. I wasn't aware I went back to sleep until I woke up to Arashi in my face screaming wake up.

"Really Arashi" I said opening my eyes to see Arashi standing in front of me with a bright ass smile on her face.

"You must have had a good dream the way you were moaning and talking in your sleep." Arashi said as she walked away from me to sit on the couch in front of me.

"WHAT! I was not." I said to Arashi with my mouth wide open in surprise.

"Umm, yes you were. You kept saying Nathaniel name. Were you having a wet dream about Nathaniel?" Arashi asked sitting up eager to get me to talk.

I opened my mouth to say something and then stopped when I saw Nathaniel standing on the steps.

"Come on Adena. Give me some details on the dream you were having about Nathaniel. It sounded hot the way you were moaning." Arashi said wondering why I didn't respond to her question the first time.

I looked at her and mentally told her to shut up because Nathaniel was behind her standing on the stairs. Arashi mentally said oops and got up to walk to the kitchen with a huge smile on her face. I couldn't look at Nathaniel after that so I got my glass and took it in the kitchen to join Arashi and Bruce.

Chapter Nine

For the next few days we practiced hard. Preparing
ourselves for whatever awaits us when we go get
Quentin. Bruce decided to make the practice a little
different today. We had to learn to control our
emotions for each other so the first practice battle was
Arashi and Joel. This is the first time I ever seen
Arashi not happy about practice. She didn't want to
hurt Joel and Joel didn't want to hurt Arashi. Because
of their feelings for each other it makes them a target
for each other. Bruce wanted us to trust that even the
ones we care for can hold their own just as we can
hold our own.

Arashi and Joel went to stand in the center of the
circle Bruce created as our battle field. They stood
about 10 feet apart. Arashi gave Joel a shy low smile

and Joel gave her a series nod in return. Both Arashi and Joel got ready for the battle but neither one went into their normal stance.

Bruce stood between them, nodded to each one of them and then said begin. It took a minute for the battle to begin because they just stood there holding each other's gaze. Finally Arashi charged towards Joel at normal speed at first and then went full on speed towards Joel. Joel didn't move while he watched and waited for her to come to him. When Arashi made it to Joel she leaped wrapping her legs around him, restraining his arms down and smiled at Joel.

Arashi twisted trying to throw Joel but Joel held his unbreakable stance preventing Arashi from throwing him. Joel moved his arms up to grip Arashi at her waist and then slammed her straight down to the ground. Arashi hit the ground so hard I felt it under my feet. I wanted to go after Joel but Arashi mentally stopped me, looking at me saying no. I froze in place using every strength I had to not charge Joel.

Arashi is now aware that Joel wasn't going to go easy on her and it was indeed going to be a real battle.

Using full strength, Arashi flipped back giving Joel a full blow to the face with her knees. Joel flipped back landing on his feet. Arashi remained in a crouch position holding Joel gaze.

She charged again full speed this time blinking out coming behind Joel, kicking him in the spine. Joel twisted in the mist of flying forward and grabbed Arashi still extended leg bringing her down with him. Arashi landed in a split while Joel landed in a crouched position on his knee still holding Arashi leg.

Arashi flipped forward with her left leg barely missing Joel as he flipped away rolling on his feet. Arashi flipped up as Joel rushed towards her giving her a blow to the stomach sending her flying. Arashi hit a tree in the forest causing the tree to fall, vibrating the ground when it finally touched down. Joel didn't miss a beat as he charged full speed towards Arashi. Arashi waited till the last minute to leap up in the trees hiding herself within the branches. Joel leaped to follow Arashi but was cut short when Arashi swung from one of the branches knocking Joel back down to hit the ground full force cracking the ground around him.

Arashi Landed next to Joel as he started to rise kicking him back across the battle field. Before Joel landed Arashi went full speed towards Joel blinking out of sight to come behind him but with an unexpected turn Joel grabbed Arashi turning her in a complete 360 before finally slamming her to the ground.

Before Joel can release her, Arashi wrapped her legs around Joel underarm and neck and slammed him down next to her on the ground. They struggled trying to overcome each other going tic for tact in each blow they gave. They finally broke free of each other, rolling away and getting on their feet. Both Arashi and Joel were breathing hard but trying not to show any sign of defeat.

They both charged towards each other with so much speed that when they crashed into each other we all felt it in the wind. Joel took a few steps back catching his balance as Arashi flew back towards the broken tree trunk she created earlier. Joel seen where Arashi was going to land and immediately leaped after her to stop her from hitting the tree trunk.

As Joel made it to Arashi, Arashi instincts kicked in

and she twisted out of Joel reach and flipped back landing on her feet as Joel took the hit to the tree truck. Joel landed on one of the pointed pieces that went through his side. We all gasped in that moment hoping Joel was okay. Arashi rushed to his side as well as Nathaniel. I followed behind Nathaniel to make sure Joel was ok and not badly hurt. Joel slowly got up informing everybody he is ok.

"I am so sorry Joel. I didn't mean to..." Arashi started to say before she was interrupted by Nathaniel.

"What the hell was that? He was trying to save you Arashi." Nathaniel said with so much anger in his tone.

"It's ok Nathaniel. I'm fine. Arashi was just following her instincts. It was a battle after all. She wasn't supposed to trust me." Joel said trying to calm Nathaniel down.

"I'm sorry Joel. I was too wrapped up in the battle. I didn't notice what you were doing until the last minute. I'm so sorry." Arashi said.

"It's ok Arashi I'm fine." Joel said.

"The hell it is." Nathaniel said not taking his eyes of

Arashi.

"Nathaniel." I said his name as I reached out to him to try to get his attention but Nathaniel knocked my hand away.

"Don't." Nathaniel said struggling to hold his anger in while watching Arashi.

Joel stepped in front of Arashi to block her view from Nathaniel. Joel stood in a strong stance with his face intense not taking his eyes off Nathaniel.

"Arashi move away." Joel told Arashi without taking his eyes of Nathaniel.

I went to Arashi side to pull her away. I looked up at Nathaniel and noticed that his eyes had started to change. His eyes was almost completely grey. I couldn't believe he was this angry over an accident. I pushed Arashi behind me trying to put more distance between her and Nathaniel.

"This is crazy. It was an accident Nathaniel." Arashi said before she turned and walked away rolling her eyes.

That's all it took for Nathaniel to lose control of his anger. He stepped forward and Joel met his step to try and stop him but Nathaniel pushed Joel without even flexing a muscle. I was next in line blocking Arashi from Nathaniel.

Arashi had already made it half way across the battle field when she heard Joel hit the ground after Nathaniel pushed him out the way. Nathaniel had walked around me since I did nothing to try and stop him. Arashi rushed to be by Joel side but was suddenly blocked by Nathaniel sudden flash in front of her.

I saw Nathaniel hand go back so I ran full speed and made it in front of Arashi to stop Nathaniel but as my hands went in the air to yield Nathaniel from his attack, I intersected his blow to the stomach that sent me flying into Arashi and us both flying and slamming into the house. In that instant Nathaniel snapped out of his rage when he noticed he hurt me instead of Arashi. He froze and his mouth dropped open. I can see he wanted to say something but nothing came out.

"Nathaniel, I'm ok." I said as I got up off Arashi.

"The hell you are." Arashi said infuriated at Nathaniel.

"I didn't intentionally hurt Joel but you intended to hurt me and in the process hurt Adena." Arashi yelled at Nathaniel walking towards him.

"Arashi no. I'm fine. This won't make anything better if we keep attacking each other." I said now blocking Arashi from Nathaniel. I really have to stop getting in the middle of people rage.

"Arashi don't." Joel said pulling Arashi into his embrace.

"Joel are you ok?" Arashi asked Joel falling into his distraction.

"I'm fine. Feel like cleaning me up since you are responsible for my battle wound?" Joel asked smiling at Arashi to lighten her mood.

"Yes. Sorry again." Arashi told Joel with a shy smile on her face.

"It's ok. Come on." Joel said leading Arashi back in the house.

"Joel." Nathaniel called out.

"It's ok Nathaniel." Joel said turning around to face Nathaniel. They both gave each other a nod and Joel turned to go back to the house.

"Bruce can we take a minute." I asked so that I can recover from the blow to my stomach. I thought I was ok but that blow really affected me a little.

"Of course." Bruce said.

I walked back to the house avoiding eye contact with Nathaniel. I just wanted to make it to my room. I walked in the door and was thankful that Arashi and Joel was not downstairs. I took the stairs two at a time and rushed to my room. I went straight to my bed and laid back to catch my breath. I felt uneasy so I went in the bathroom to throw water on my face but ended up running to the toilet to hurl.

I finally felt a jolt of pain where I was hit by Nathaniel. I walked over to the mirror and lifted my shirt to see Nathaniel's fist print almost embedded into my stomach. I knew he hit me hard but I wasn't aware how much power he put into that hit until now. While examining the brush I was interrupted my Nathaniel.

"Adena...... I'm sorry............ I didn't want to hurt you." Nathaniel said shocked by the bruise on my stomach.

"Well you did. Why did you get so angry? Joel is perfectly able to handle himself." I snapped at Nathaniel.

"I'm sorry. I.......I........I'll just leave you alone."
Nathaniel said turning to leave.

"So you just going to leave? Look at me Nathaniel.
You're not leaving until you tell me why you got so
angry." I demanded.

"I don't know. I guess I am still protective of Joel.
I......I still see my little brother being held down and
burned and I wasn't there to stop it before it
happened."

"Nathaniel, Joel is far from being that scared little boy.
You were so angry and could have done a lot worse.
I'm glad I blocked you from hitting Arashi."

"I'm not." Nathaniel snapped walking over to me. He
touched the bruise on my stomach and I took a deep
breath because it hurt.

"It's not that bad. I'm sure it'll heal soon." I said
stepping back away from Nathaniel and pulling my
shirt back down.

"I'm sorry Adena. I never want to hurt you."
Nathaniel said and closed the distance between us. He
lifted my shirt back up, rubbed his hand across my
bruise again and then kissed it. "Better."

"What the hell did you do?" Arashi said standing in the doorway looking at the bruise on my stomach. I snatched my shirt back down and walked over to Arashi.

"Arashi it's okay. It will heal soon." I said trying to defuse Arashi.

"Adena, that really looks bad. Is that why you threw up? I felt you throw up and came in here to check on you." Arashi said putting me on the spot.

"WHAT!" Nathaniel said looking horrified by the news.

"Yes. You hit Adena so hard, there's no telling what you did to her." Arashi snapped at Nathaniel.

"Adena you said it didn't hurt." Nathaniel held my gaze waiting for my response.

"Well she lied." Arashi snapped back at Nathaniel.

"Arashi can you give us a minute?" I asked before she made it even more uncomfortable then it already was.

"He hits you and I'm the one who has to leave." Arashi said looking at me crazy like I went back to my abusive husband or something.

"Really Arashi. I think your pushing it a little." I said

with a little amusement on my face.

"Maybe. Maybe not." Arashi said taking her leave but not before she gave Nathaniel her evil look.

"I'm sorry. Arashi can be over protective at times." I said heading back into my room. It was uncomfortable standing in the bathroom now.

"Adena you should have told me I hurt you that bad." Nathaniel snapped at me.

"I'm fine Nathaniel. Calm down." I said brushing him off. I just want to lay down and close my eyes.

"Lay down. I'll go get some ice." Nathaniel ordered walking out my room.

"I'm fine. All I want to do is lay down." I said laying back on my bed and closing my eyes.

"Then lay down while I put ice on this bruise." Nathaniel said returning sooner than I expected. These abilities of ours is starting to become a headache.

I winced at the cool ice against my stomach. I wasn't use to being taking care of. I never needed it before. Arashi and I never been in a fight where we didn't win or where we were not the strongest.

I didn't open my eyes to look at Nathaniel because I

didn't want the uncomfortable feeling I have around him to kick in. But for some reason Nathaniel always seemed to know what I'm thinking.

"I know I make you uncomfortable." Nathaniel said adjusting the ice on my bruise. I froze, opening my eyes to look at him. How in the hell does he know that.

"Breathe Adena." Nathaniel said catching my gaze.

"How do you know you make me uncomfortable?" I asked wanting to know how he always know what I'm thinking.

"Your body language. It always give you away." Nathaniel said with a slight smile on his face.

"I……..I…….." I was stuttering not knowing what to say until I was cut off by Nathaniel.

"I wouldn't make you so uncomfortable if you just admit to yourself you feel something for me." Nathaniel said with a more intense look on his face now.

"It's not that simple Nathaniel. I don't know or understand why I have feelings for you." I said being honest.

"Why do you need a reason to feel what you feel Adena?" Nathaniel asked. I had a feeling he already know the answer to that question.

"I love Quentin Nathaniel. I already feel bad about what happened in the shower when I should have been concentrating on getting Quentin back." I said now mad for bringing the shower scene up.

"Ah… so you're mad because you let go in your time of need when you feel like you should have only been thinking about Quentin." Nathaniel stated.

"No……Yes……I guess." I said confused about his understanding.

"Adena I'm not going to stop coming for you. After we get Quentin back, I'm letting you know now I will make it hard for you to choose him. I won't hold back like I am now." Nathaniel said holding my gaze.

"What do you mean holding back now? Nathaniel do you think you can have me whenever you want?" I asked.

"Yes Adena. I can." He said with pure confidence in voice.

"That's ridiculous Nathaniel. I'm not at your beck and

call. You don't control whether I give myself to you or not." I snapped at Nathaniel.

"Adena you may not want to admit to yourself that you want me. But you do and I will have you Adena. I'm just letting you know I won't wait much longer and I won't sit back and watch you be another man." Nathaniel said not letting go of my gaze.

My mouth dropped open to his words. I couldn't believe he was being so bold about it. I do have feelings for Nathaniel but it can be some freaky version of whatever it is we supposed to be. I'm not giving in to him and I want him to know that. I closed my mouth and set up on my arms to let Nathaniel know it wasn't going to be that easy for him but before I can speak, Nathaniel grabbed my wrist pulling my arms forward making me fall back down in a laying position and covered my body with his. He slowly let his body weight from the waist down push me further into the bed. I felt every inch of his still rising cock against my folds.

I gasps at how big his dick was and tried to contain myself from wrapping my legs around him. As usual it was like Nathaniel knew actually what I was thinking and used his legs to spread my legs apart and used his right hand to lift my leg around him. He did the same thing with my other leg then pressed me further into the bed with his dick feeling like it was about to rip through my jeans, enter my pussy and fuck me without a single move from Nathaniel.

My mind is trying to fight the overload of feelings I'm having and I almost did until Nathaniel started to move in a circular motion against my now tender clit and forced a moan out of me. I couldn't believe I was losing this mental battle Nathaniel was playing with me. I knew he was proving his point but I still refuse to yield to him.

Before I knew it Nathaniel was kissing me very patiently and then he got ruff. His tongue fought through my lips and entwined with my tongue forcing me to participate in his seduction. I couldn't help myself. I put my hands in Nathaniel hair and let go of my stubbornness kissing him back. I noticed Nathaniel had stopped and pulled back stopping our kiss.

I opened my eyes and he was just staring down at me

with an intense smile on his face. I accepted my defeat. I cannot deny Nathaniel. I want him and I want him bad. I could tell it took a lot for him to pull away from me as he slowly raised off me. He got up to leave and I didn't want him to leave. I tried reminding myself of Quentin but the vision of Nathaniel right now is forbidding me.

"Nathaniel." I called out his name with so much need and passion in my voice.

"Adena let me go. If I stay I won't be able to stop myself from fucking the shit out of you and I won't give a damn about you feeling bad about it afterwards." Nathaniel said with so much need and want in his voice. I opened my mouth to say something but nothing came out. He was right I would feel bad afterwards but couldn't ignore how I felt right now.

"Keep the ice on your bruise." Nathaniel said not turning to face me. He begin to walk out the door but stopped because of my response.

"You're the one who wanted to ice my bruise not me." I said feeling a little irritated that he got me all hot and bothered to prove a point and didn't finish me off. "Don't fuck with me right now Adena. Put the damn ice on your bruise. I'm going to take a cold shower. Maybe you should do the same." Nathaniel snapped at me before finally making it out my room.

I laid back on my bed and did as I was instructed. I can't help but to be angry. Nathaniel just snapped at me and I'm laying here doing exactly what he told me to do. Why do I listen to him? I threw the ice off me onto my bed and got up to take a much needed shower.

I needed a cold shower but didn't want to take one because Nathaniel suggested it so I made my water lukewarm. It did not help at all. I ended up even more frustrated. I can't wait to get Quentin back. As soon as he is safe, I'm going to fuck the living day light out of him.

I got out the shower and got dressed in my usual jeans and t-shirt. I went down stairs to get something to eat. I knew Bruce had something cooked up because I am starving. When I made it down stairs everyone was already there. All of the sudden all eyes were on me.

"What!" I snapped at everybody and walked to the kitchen to pour myself a glass of juice.

"What's up with the attitude Adena? We just want to make sure you're okay." Arashi said.

"I'm fine." I snapped again. Arashi mentally asked me am I okay and I snapped at her *"back off"*.

"Sorry." I said realizing I took it too far. It wasn't her fault I was sexually frustrated.

"It's okay. I guess we need to get Quentin back sooner than later." Arashi said teasing me.

"You guys think you ready for another practice round before we lose the daylight?" Bruce asked.

"Yes." I stated being the first to rush out the door. Everyone came out behind me and headed back to the battle field. We all stood in a circle around the field waiting to see who Bruce will call next to battle.

"Adena and Nathaniel please step onto the battle field." Bruce said.

I looked at Bruce with my mouth wide open wanting to ask why I had to practice with him, but closed my mouth and stumped over into the battle field like a little girl throwing a tantrum. I heard Nathaniel laugh on his way to the battlefield making me even angrier.

"Something funny Nathaniel." I snapped at him.

"Not at all. Just enjoying the view." Nathaniel said with a grin that could light up the room.

"This should be good." I heard Dante say next to Bruce. I gave Dante a don't fuck with me look. He put his hands in the air and shrugged his shoulders at me.

"Begin." Bruce said.

I immediately snapped my focus back at Nathaniel. He still had that grin on his face and the only thing I could think of was the different ways I can knock that grin off his face. Yes. This was a satisfying thought that brought a smile to my face.

"Come on baby. Show me what you got." Nathaniel said teasing me. I was infuriated that he just called me baby. I'm not his damn baby. I charged Nathaniel wanting him to know he does not have the right to call me baby. Nathaniel met my charge and started blocking every hit and kick I sent his way. He was still smiling like he was playing with a little cat or something. I kept coming at him with more hits and kicks, faster and faster. He blocked them all twisting and turning away, blinking out behind me and tapping my shoulder. He was making me even angrier.

"Stop it Nathaniel and fight me." I snapped at him while he blocked all my attempts to hit him.

"I'm not going to fight you when you're attacking me like a crazy person. You're thinking with your anger and you will end up hurt in the process." Nathaniel said.

I stopped trying to hit Nathaniel and let out a loud frustrated scream, then stomped back into the house to get away from everybody. I went to my room and laid back on my bed trying to calm myself down. I never been this worked up before. I heard someone come in my room and I was not in the mood to be messed with.

"GET OUT!" I screamed to whoever was standing there.

"WOW! Adena it's just me." Arashi said. "What's going on with you? I never seen you like this before." Arashi asked.

"I just want to hurry up and save Quentin so that we all can get on with our lives." I said in a frustrated tone.

"Is this about Nathaniel? Did he do something else to you?" Arashi asked. Now concerned about me.

"Yes….No…..Nothing but make me sexually frustrated." I said.

"OMG! You like him Adena." Arashi said laughing at me.

"I do not." I screamed at Arashi.

"You wouldn't be this frustrated if you didn't Adena. We all can see something is going on between you two. Maybe you should figure it out before you hurry into something with Quentin and end up hurting him because you want Nathaniel." Arashi said.

"No Arashi. I love Quentin. He's my soul mate. I don't want anybody but him." I said trying to convince Arashi and myself.

"I doubt that Adena. Look at you. You never felt this way before. Not even when you went a while without getting any from Quentin. It's not just sexual frustration you have for Nathaniel. Adena you feel something for him." Arashi said trying to get me to see past my stubbornness.

"Arashi that's only because I miss Quentin. I need Quentin." I said trying to convince Arashi to see it from my side again.

"You think when we finally save Quentin your feelings for Nathaniel will go away?" Arashi asked.

"Yes…..No……Yes…..Maybe." I said now more confused than ever.

"Adena you need to except that your feelings for Nathaniel are real. And I got a feeling he's not going anywhere anytime soon honey." Arashi said with a small smile on her face.

"Now that I can believe." I said laughing at Arashi very true statement.

Nathaniel had already admitted that he wasn't going to make it easy for me after we saved Quentin. Arashi is right I need to accept that my feelings for Nathaniel is not going anywhere and he won't let me push him aside too much longer.

"Try to relax Adena. Tomorrow we will discuss strategy and prepare to go save Quentin and hopefully get some information about ourselves as well.

"Okay. Thanks Arashi." I said calming down.

"You welcome." Arashi said getting up to leave.

"By the way. When did you become team Nathaniel?" I asked since she didn't like him that much earlier.

"He's not that bad. I'm still pissed at him for hurting you but he's not a bad guy and he cares for you." Arashi said.

"Yea I guess so." I said trying to clear my thoughts.

"Don't think too hard about it Adena. You'll end up over analyzing things when it's really very simple." Arashi said then took her leave.

I tried to relax and clear my head. It wasn't really working because I started thinking about both Nathaniel and Quentin. Comparing them in my head and making a pro and con list of what I like and don't like. Which really didn't help because I don't really dislike anything about either of them. I finally dozed off and let sleep take me over.

Chapter Ten

I woke up feeling a little better this morning. I checked the bruise on my stomach and was happy to see it had healed completely. I jumped out of bed and took a long steamy shower. I realized that in just the couple of days we been here, It felt like we all been here forever. I'm happy that today we get out of here and head to sensei Arobi dojo to finally save Quentin. I hope everyone else is up so that we can talk strategy and come up with a plan. Sounds like an easy enough task but I know it will turn into a never ending debate. I got out the shower and got dressed. Today I am feeling good so I put on some skinny jeans, a royal blue croc cami top, my black knee boots and let my hair down. I feel how I look. Sexy, relaxed, and confident. I headed downstairs to get some juice.

Bruce was the only one downstairs making breakfast as usual.

"Morning Bruce." I said with a big smile on my face.

"Good Morning Adena. You're happy this morning and wow, you look nice." Bruce said taken back by my mood and outfit.

"Thanks. I feel great." I said.

"I see your stomach has healed." Bruce noticed since I decided to wear a top that shows off my abs.

"Yes it is." I smiled at Bruce and went outside to sit up in the trees and enjoy the view. I looked over all the trees in the forest and stared at the sun shining bright over us. It was beautiful out today and I hope I get to enjoy another day like this one after we save Quentin. I kept staring into the sun until I heard my name.

"Adena breakfast is ready." I heard Nathaniel say.

I swung down from one of the branches landing a short distance from Nathaniel. Nathaniel mouth dropped open as he froze in place looking me up and down.

"Ok." I smiled at Nathaniel as I walked past him into the house. I walked straight into everybody gaze. I don't dress up that much so I knew they would react this way. I just smiled and walked to have a seat at the table.

"Wow Adena. You look great." Arashi said breaking the silence.

"Thank you Arashi." I said still smiling from everyone's expressions.

"Let's eat." Bruce said as he set the food on the table.

"I take it you didn't wear that for me." Nathaniel whispered to me from the seat next to me.

"No. I'm wearing this for myself." I whispered back.

"You look beautiful Adena." Nathaniel said winning my gaze.

"Thank you." I said blushing.

Everybody ate their breakfast in peace for the next few minutes. After we were done. We cleared the table. Arashi and I washed the dishes and we went to sit with the guys in the living room when we were done. As usual Arashi went and sat on Joel lap as Nathaniel sat on the other end of that couch. Bruce and Dante was on the other couch and I sat at the end next to Dante and straight across from Nathaniel.

"What's the plan Adena?" Nathaniel said when we were finally seated.

"I hope it changed from walking to the front door and knocking." Dante said sarcastically.

"Look there's only three people who knows the ins and outs of Sensei Arobi's dojo. That's me, Arashi, and Rin. Rin has an advantage because he knows all the hidden trails. No matter what strategy we come up with, Rin would have the upper hand. So we should make him think he won." I said trying to get to the point.

"How do we do that without getting caught?" Joel asked.

"By letting Rin have what he want." Nathaniel answered looking at me.

"Yes." I responded back to Nathaniel.

"No. There has to be another way." Nathaniel snapped.

"There isn't." Arashi said looking to Joel.

"We will be fine Nathaniel." I said trying to ease his mood.

"You don't know that Adena. You're putting yourself

in danger not knowing for sure what his plan is."
Nathaniel snapped not calming down.

"He's right Adena. My father will be prepared for
every possibility." Dante said.

"Your father only knows about me, you, and Arashi.
He knows nothing about Nathaniel and Joel or
Bruce." I said to Dante.

"Bruce? Why would my father be worried about
Bruce?" Dante asked looking just as confused as
everyone else does by my statement.

"Bruce wasn't just Sensei Arobi trusted friend. He was
his brother. Bruce training is much greater than any
one would expect." I said answering everyone's
questions. I been going over Bruce involvement in me,
Arashi, and Arobi's life since I decided to go pay him a
visit the day we met Dante. There always seemed to be
more to Sensei Arobi and Bruce story.

"How did you know?" Bruce asked me. He wasn't
surprised that I figured it out and he didn't deny it
either.

"When Arashi and I were kids, after we would finish
with training we would go play in the forest flipping in

and out of the trees. One time when we were swinging around on the branches, one of the branches I swung off of broke and I fell down near the back of the dojo. I saw you and Arobi training so I decided to watch. The training was intense and the moves you and Arobi used were nothing like the ones taught to Arashi and I. I watched until the end when Arobi came at you with his most powerful move and it was like you deflected it using the air around you. Your move was so powerful it pushed Arobi away sending him flying through the wind and pulling me forward like I was being yanked from an actual person without you even laying a hand on Arobi. When you and Arobi were done training, Arobi bowed and said to you one day big brother and you responded one day little brother.

I didn't know what that meant back then, but now I understand. You loved Arobi as only a brother would and you took care of him only as a big brother would for his little brother. I realized it after the battle practice yesterday. How Nathaniel is so protective over Joel and the expression of understanding you had after everything had happened." I said explaining to Bruce how I found out about him and Arobi.

"Why didn't you tell me?" Arashi asked a little disappointed that I kept it from her.

"I didn't think anything of it at the time and we were so young. I didn't understand what I saw or felt." I explained to Arashi.

"You have always been a smart girl Adena. It is true. Arobi was my little brother. I taught him everything he knew after our father died. Arobi was very young when our father died so I stepped up and guided him the best way I could. He was the best brother I could ever ask for." Bruce said remembering back to his time with Arobi.

"Well that's something my father doesn't know. WOW!" Dante said stunned by the news.

"How do you plan on using that?" Nathaniel said not missing a beat.

"Hopefully we won't have to. Rin is expecting me, Arashi and Dante. Arashi and I will go in using the hidden trails we know while Dante take the trails that only Rin knows about. We will take out majority of what Rin has waiting for us before getting caught." I started to explain.

"Then you and Joel can come save us." Arashi said smiling at Joel.

"Assuming we don't get caught." Joel said

"What makes you think we won't get caught using the same trails you and Arashi are using?" Nathaniel asked.

"That's where Bruce comes in at. We assume that only Rin knows the ins and outs of the dojo but that's not true. Arobi only trusted the scrolls location to one person and would have only hid the one scroll that explain everything in one place that only one person can find it and that's Bruce." Directing my attention on Bruce I explained what I needed Bruce to do.

"Bruce we need you to get Nathaniel and Joel in unnoticed. You are the only person who can. Rin knows nothing about them so we have a slight advantage if they are not caught with us." I said holding Bruce's gaze.

"I understand." Bruce said.

"Will you help us?" Arashi asked.

"It will be my honor." Bruce smiled at us.

Bruce decided to draw a map of the dojo and the land

around it. Him and Dante filled in the hidden trails and went through different scenarios for us to try. Nathaniel and Joel studied the map while Bruce and Dante went over and over it. Bruce kept his and Arobi's secret trail to himself. He said that it was a secret only for him and Arobi and when the time is right he will pass its location on.

We all scattered to get our stuff together for the journey to Arobi's dojo. We didn't need much. It's in everybody best interest to pack light. I went to my room to pack my black leggings, black tank top and black combat boots. I packed my toothbrush, grabbed my passport and some money for the trip. I was interrupted by a knock on my door so I turned around expecting it to be Nathaniel but it wasn't.

"You have a minute?" Joel asked.

"Of course Joel." I said still shocked to see him at my door.

"I just wanted to thank you for accepting me and Nathaniel. We would not have had the opportunity to find out more about ourselves if it wasn't for you and Arashi." Joel stated.

"Oh Joel you don't have to thank me. You and Nathaniel have brought us the same opportunity. Without you, Arashi and I would still be in the dark about who or what we are." I said.

"You opened your doors up to us and you didn't have to. You could have sent us on our way instead of helping us. You and Arashi are a blessing to us. I love Arashi very much and I can see Nathaniel has strong feelings for you as well. We will forever be in your debt. I just wanted to let you know that. Thank you." Joel said.

"You welcome." I replied with an acknowledging smile on my face.

Joel nodded and took his leave. I sat on my bed and took a deep breath. I gathered my things and headed down stairs to meet everybody.

Chapter Eleven

We arrived at O'Hare Airport two hours early so we can get our tickets and check in our bags with no problems. Although we all lived a sort of lucrative life before we were suddenly distracted from our normal routines, we all are well off financially so we decided to go first class since the journey is so long. It only cost $51,718.20 for all our tickets which wasn't that bad since Arashi spends more than that on one shopping spree.

Arashi and I own a private security company that cater to mostly rich people needs. A lot of our clients are CEO's and others acquire our service for their illegal business or private lives. This is Chicago after all. Almost everything done here is illegal.

While Arashi handled the security part being the face of the company, I handled all the investments. We make a substantial amount of money that allows us to enjoy life instead of just making it through. Nathaniel and Joel made a great deal of money being hit man or ninja's as some of their clients prefer to think of them as. It's amazing how many high paying clients they have.

Chicago is a good place to become rich off of crime. Nathaniel is usually the one to get his hands dirty since he still feels the need to protect Joel. I wonder when we get back will Nathaniel loosen up on Joel a little. Dante on the other hand did not need money. He was practically his father prisoner all these years. He had what Rin wanted him to have.

As for Bruce, he lived off his family money. They made quite a bit running their family dojo. Sensei Arobi ran the dojo and from time to time Bruce kept Arobi on his toes with their private training sessions I guess. Bruce also opened his own flower boutique. Bruce always loved nature and like sharing his knowledge of flowers and where they come from with his customers. Don't be mistaken, some of those flowers cost a lot to acquire. I guess we all have a pretty good life, except for Dante. Maybe he would come back with us and start a new life here with us. We got our tickets and went to the first class lounge to relax until our flight was ready. Everyone seem to take advantage of the amenities except for me. I couldn't stop thinking about Quentin. How is he, if Rin hurt him, will he be alive when we get to him or if we all are heading into a suicide mission.

"Don't worry. We'll get Quentin back." Nathaniel said sitting next to me noticing my anxiousness.

"How do you do that?" I asked wondering once again how he always know what I'm thinking.

"I told you......" Nathaniel started to say.

"My body language gives me away." I said finishing his sentence.

"Yes." He said with a low smile on his face.

"Thank you." I said hiding my face so he won't see me blush.

"For?" Nathaniel said lifting my face up so he can see me.

"Helping us get Quentin back. I know this has got to be a little weird for you." I said gazing into his eyes.

"What? Helping the woman I desire save the man she loves. Not weird at all. I bet lots of men do it every day." Nathaniel said goofing around.

"Yea right." I said laughing. I was really laughing hard and I noticed I haven't did that in a while.

"You helped me find information about my family. It's the least I can do." Nathaniel said running his finger over my cheek.

"Helping you get information about your family wasn't a suicide mission Nathaniel." I said pointing out the difference in our situations.

"Neither is this Adena. We're going up against some ninja's who don't know much about us. It may not feel like it but we still have the upper hand." Nathaniel said comforting me.

"We can't underestimate Rin. He wouldn't be luring us there if he didn't have something up his sleeve. I can feel it. Something is just not right with this." I said losing myself in my thoughts.

"We will deal with it when it comes." Nathaniel said

entwining his fingers in mine.

I took a deep breath when I heard the attendant come and tell us we can board now. We all grabbed our stuff and headed to board the plane. First class was so much easier. No hassle and spacious.

Our flight is 18 hours and 35 minutes. We only have to make one stop. Since we were lucky to get an early flight, our departure time is 7:25 a.m. and we should land in Tokyo by 4 p.m. tomorrow. It's a nice village close to where Bruce lived before coming to Chicago. Bruce place is nice but we decided to get a hotel room just in case Rin has Bruce place being watched. I relaxed in my seat and waited for the attendant to bring my juice. I prefer apple juice but I ordered orange juice. As I waited, I looked around at everybody.

They all seemed happy. We looked like we been together all our life. We learned a lot about each other these past few days. I have to admit it's been nice having other people around and I'm glad Arashi found someone she really cares about. I stared at Arashi and Joel and saw how happy they were. I smiled at the sight of them two.

"You know he really loves you." I said to Arashi using our connection.

"I Know." Arashi smiled catching my gaze.

"I'm happy for you. You deserve it." I told Arashi.

"So do you Adena. Nathaniel loves you too. I can see it in his eyes each time he looks at you." Arashi said.

"Arashi I love Quentin. I don't know Nathaniel like I know Quentin. I.....I....I can't believe that he truly loves me when we only known each other a short time." I said dropping my gaze and frowning my face.

"Adena you just said Joel truly loves me. We met them at the same time. You don't want to accept it because you love Quentin. It is okay to hold on to his love but don't dismiss Nathaniel feelings because you're scared he might actually be your true love. Think about it Adena. You really do feel something for him." Arashi said trying to get me to open my eyes.

"I do feel something for Nathaniel. I just don't know why." I said returning my gaze back to Arashi.

"Adena there won't be a logical reason for everything. You feel what you feel. Stop fighting it and see where it takes you." Arashi said.

"I can't think about this now Arashi. We're on our way to save Quentin." I said not wanting to think about my feelings for Nathaniel right now.

"Just saying Adena. If Nathaniel is anything like Joel in bed you won't be thinking about Quentin that much longer anyway." Arashi said smiling at Joel.

"ARASHI!" I said dropping my mouth wide open at her statement.

"What are you two talking about? Adena you look like you just had a baby or something." Dante said.

"I was just telling Adena if........." Arashi started to say before I cut her off.

"Nothing." I snapped glaring at Arashi. Arashi laughed and gave Nathaniel a wink before returning her gaze back to Joel.

"Do I want to know?" Nathaniel asked me.

"No. Arashi was just fooling around." I answered.

"Not yet I'm not." Arashi said flirting with Joel.

"Okay kids. We have a long road ahead of us. Get some rest." Bruce said.

Bruce was right. We all needed to rest. I closed my eyes not really tired but anxious to get there. My thoughts were all over the place. The only thing that kept going through my head was images of Quentin and images of Nathaniel. Finally I drifted off to sleep but my thoughts followed me into my dreams. I was in a beautiful home surrounded with laughter and love. The problem is that although I'm in the mist of it, it's far from my reach. No matter what direction I go in, there's a clear wall stopping me from reaching my wants and needs. Suddenly I see Quentin reaching out to me and I smiled and reached for him but right before I reached him I am jolted back by something. I turned to see my hands entwined with Nathaniel. He's being so patient waiting for me. I turned my focus back to Quentin to see his still extended hand reaching out for me. I reached for him but the rest of my body would not move from this one spot. I stretched a little further and finally got my finger tips to touch his but was immediately yanked back from Nathaniel. I was torn between the two. I looked back and forth between the two until at the same time they both dropped their hands.

I felt free to make my choice so I leaped into the arms

of Quentin. When I turned to face Nathaniel he
nodded and walked away. My heart jumped out of my
chest and I dropped to my knees. I screamed for
Nathaniel not to go anywhere. Not to leave me. But he
kept walking away.

"Adena wake up, wake up Adena." Nathaniel snapped
shaking me out my sleep.

"NO!" I screamed waking up out of my sleep to see all
eyes on me. Everybody was looking back and forth
from me to Nathaniel. Nathaniel was standing over me
with an intense look on his face. He looked like he
wanted to do something but couldn't. Like he was
helpless and didn't want to accept that feeling.

"Adena you okay? Must have been some dream."
Arashi said always stating the obvious.

"Yes." I said to Arashi not dropping my gaze from
Nathaniel.

Nathaniel walked away and went to sit back in his seat.
He looked furious. What the hell did I say in my sleep
to piss him off? Before I could ask, an announcement
was made saying we would be landing soon. I didn't
realize I slept that long.

We were landing in Tokyo, Japan. When the plane landed we all gathered our things and headed off the plane. We had a car waiting to take us to the hotel. We booked three deluxe rooms at The Conrad. Arashi got one for her and Joel, One is for me, and the other is for Bruce, Dante and Nathaniel.

When we made it to the hotel, we got our room keys and headed to the rooms. I said someone can stay in my room if they like hoping Nathaniel will so I can ask him what I said to make him so angry but he paid me no attention and went in the room with Bruce and Dante. Arashi looked at me and shrugged her shoulders then pulled Joel to their room. I was the last one still standing in the hallway.

I finally went to my room and threw my bag down on the floor. The room was beautiful with a bay view. I sat in the chair and just gazed out the window. Tomorrow we will finally be going to save Quentin and maybe all my confusion will be over.

I heard a knock at my door and got up to answer it. I opened the door and it was Nathaniel storming past me and pacing back and forth in my room. I closed the door and walked over to him.

"What the hell was that Adena?" Nathaniel snapped at me stopping me in my tracks.

"What was what Nathaniel? Why are you so angry?" I asked confused about what's going on.

"You keep saying you want Quentin, you love Quentin, he's your soul mate but you beg me not to leave you in a fucking dream. That scream. You screamed like somebody was ripping your soul out your body." Nathaniel said still pacing back and forth.

"I'm sorry Nathaniel. I'm not trying to confuse you. I just......" I was saying until Nathaniel cut me off.

"You just want what Adena? If you say Quentin I'm going to.......this won't end well." Nathaniel said warning me.

"That's not what I was going to say Nathaniel. You need to calm down. I don't understand why you're so angry." I said again confused by his anger.

"You don't understand." Nathaniel said laughing. "I care for you Adena. I will never leave you or hurt you the way you were hurting in that dream. For god sakes I'm here with you trying to save your damn boyfriend.

I never felt so helpless in my life. Not even when...." Nathaniel stopped in the mist of his sentence.

"When Joel was attacked by your adopted parents." I said finishing his sentence.

"Adena what do you want?" Nathaniel asked walking up to me.

"I don't know. Nathaniel I have feelings for you but I love Quentin. I'm here for Quentin" I said walking backwards away from Nathaniel.

"What do you want Adena?" Nathaniel asked again now face to face with me.

"Nathaniel I don't know. Please don't do this now. I can't." I said again walking back and hitting the wall. Nathaniel had me now. He pushed his body against mine forcing me to feel his presence.

"Nathaniel Please." I said looking away. I didn't want to face him while he was this close to me.

"I won't ask again Adena. What do you want?" Nathaniel said grabbing my chin and making me look into his eyes.

"I.....I.....I want you Nathaniel. I want you to take me. To love me and make all this shit go away." I said giving in to my feelings.

"See that wasn't hard." Nathaniel said right before kissing me. His kiss was so intense and passionate. He pressed me further into the wall, kissing me harder. I grabbed the back of his head pulling him into me more. I pushed up against him freeing one leg and then the other. When I finally got them free, I wrapped my arms around his neck, lifted myself and wrapped my legs around his waist.

Nathaniel pushed me back into the wall, pressing deeper into me. I felt his dick rising against my clit and I moaned. I didn't think it was possible but Nathaniel pushed his body further into mine and released a low moan cocking his head back. When he brought his gaze back to me his eyes had changed a little. They were grey. They looked like his natural color but filled with need. Nathaniel pushed his hands into the walls and pulled back off the wall.

"Go." Nathaniel said with a growl in his voice.

"Nathaniel." I said not understanding why he's holding back.

"I won't do this while you're still confused Adena. Go

now before I lose my control." Nathaniel said.

I couldn't tear myself away from him. I strengthened my hold around his neck and tightened my legs around his waist and begin to move up and down against his dick. I held his gaze letting him know I know what I'm doing and I want him now. I felt him tense and struggle to hold back. He let out a loud moan and slammed us back into the wall pushing his dick so far into me that I forgot we had pants on. I tilted my head back and moaned riding him harder.

"Please Nathaniel." I said pleading for him to take me now. I wished I never opened my mouth because the next thing I knew, Nathaniel pulled back, unwrapped my legs from around his waist, and caressed my cheek.

"I promise one day." Nathaniel said throwing me completely off.

"No, no, no, no, no Nathaniel. You can't leave me like this. You can't make me confess I want you then leave me like this. You can't." I said pissed that Nathaniel is doing this to me again. He proved his point and I am tired of waiting.

"Shh." Nathaniel said then he kissed me. He pushed

me back into the wall and kissed me hard. I was back in motion wrapping my hands tighter around his neck trying to pull him closer to me. Nathaniel stopped me by using his hand to push me back. He slid his hand slowly into my pants and into my panties.

He used his middle finger to push through my folds and press hard on my clit. The feeling was so sensational a low like growl escaped from my throat. He pushed in harder on my clit and moved in a circular motion. I pushed my head back into the wall moaning and moaning. Nathaniel moved his middle finger from my clit and pushed it into my folds and used his thumb to continue a tortuous rhythm on my clit.

"Please Nathaniel. I want you." I said begging him to put his dick in me instead of his fingers.

"I know baby. Come for me. Come for me like this." Nathaniel said intensifying the pleasure on my clit. I couldn't take no more. I cocked my head back and convulsed. Nathaniel gave my clit on last squeeze and I went into a shaking explosion. It took me a minute to stop shaking so Nathaniel carried me and put me in my bed.

"Go to sleep now." Nathaniel said then turned away.

"Nathaniel don't go. Lay with me." I pleaded.

"Are you sure?" Nathaniel asked.

"Yes….." I stuttered.

Nathaniel jumped in the bed with me and pulled me close to him. I was still shaking a little but calmed down when Nathaniel hold got tighter. Next thing I know I drifted off to sleep.

Chapter Twelve

The sun shining through my window woke me up. I stretched out and suddenly popped my eyes open realizing where I was. I jumped out of bed and ran into the bathroom to take a shower. The only thing I could think about was Quentin. We're going to save Quentin today. My shower was brief. I dried myself off, dropped the towel on the floor and headed back to my room.

I went directly to my bag and pulled out my black leggings, black tank top, and noticed I packed my all black lace panties and matching bra. What was I thinking? This was not the time to be sexy. I pushed the nagging I was mentally giving myself to the side and put them on.

"Nice view." Nathaniel said making me jump from his

sudden presence.

"Shit! Um yes. The bay view is beautiful." I responded.

"That wasn't the view I was talking about but yes that view is beautiful as well." Nathaniel said making me blush.

"Um thank you." I said almost tripping over my pants trying to hurry and put them on.

"Did you forget I was here Adena?" Nathaniel asked walking towards me.

"No. I just wanted to get dress so that we can get this day over with." I said walking back into the bathroom to brush out my hair.

"Yes. To save Quentin. I'll leave you alone to finish getting dressed. I'll go back to my room and take a shower." Nathaniel said heading towards the door.

"Nathaniel don't." I said not wanting to feel guilty about saving Quentin.

"Don't what Adena?" Nathaniel asked walking into the bathroom.

"Don't make me feel guilty about wanting to save Quentin." I snapped back.

"I just said I will go to my room to get dress so you

can finish getting dressed. It's obvious you're uncomfortable with me being here." Nathaniel said.

"I'm not uncomfortable. I don't want to hurt you or Quentin and I don't want to be pressured to choose between the man I love and......" I started to say and stopped myself before finishing my sentence. "Don't go Nathaniel. Stay. You can get dressed here." I said instead and then walked past Nathaniel out the bathroom. Nathaniel grabbed my hand stopping me. I looked up at him returning his gaze. I can tell he was searching my eyes to see what I was feeling. He let my hand go and nodded then went in the bathroom to get in the shower.

I ordered breakfast and headed to Bruce and Dante room to get Nathaniel bag. I figured it was the least I can do after the uncomfortable moment we just had. "Morning Bruce. Hi Dante." I said when Bruce let me in.

"Good morning Adena. How's Nathaniel? Is he feeling better?" Bruce asked.

"I think so. He's in the shower. I came to get his bags so he can get dressed." I stated knowing exactly how it sounded. I left it like that not wanting to explain if or if we didn't sleep together. Bruce pointed to Nathaniel bags and I grabbed them and went back to my room. Nathaniel was already out the shower wearing just a towel around his waist. I couldn't help but stare. His body was so perfect and masculine. It was hard to concentrate on what I wanted to say.

"I brought your bags so that you can get dressed." I said after clearing my throat.

"Thank you. That had to be weird for you." Nathaniel said smiling at me cocking his head to the side.

"A little. I also ordered breakfast. It should be here shortly." I said blushing and turning around to avoid looking at Nathaniel.

"Okay." Nathaniel said. I could hear the humor in his tone as I walked away.

Housekeeping came with our breakfast. I let them in so that they can set it out on the table. When they were done I tipped and thanked them for their services. Nathaniel came and joined me at the table. We ate in silence for a moment.

"Adena I know you are in a hurry to get Quentin back.

Just be careful." Nathaniel said with concern in his eyes.

"I will." I said.

After we finished breakfast we met everybody in Bruce room. It was time to go over the plan one last time and finally go save Quentin. Arashi, I and Dante will leave together as planned and Bruce, Nathaniel and Joel will make their way to get the scrolls. Hopefully when we meet back up everything would have went as planned and we will be heading back home with Quentin safe. We said our goodbye's and hoped that everything goes well. Arashi kissed and hugged Joel, I hugged Bruce and told him to be safe. Arashi came and hugged Bruce while Dante, Joel, and Nathaniel gave each other an acknowledging nod. Arashi hugged Nathaniel and said see you soon with a huge grin on her face. Bruce hugged Dante and last it came to me and Nathaniel. I gave Nathaniel a nod not really sure what to do. Nathaniel grabbed me and pulled me into his embrace hugging me tight.

"Be careful." Nathaniel told me looking down at me with an intense look in his eyes.

"Don't worry I'll bring her back to you in one piece."
Arashi said laughing.

"Let's go." Dante said not wanting to be a part of our weird moment.

I looked at Nathaniel and nodded then walked away.

Chapter Thirteen

Kyoto is five hours and thirty four minutes away from Tokyo. Arashi, Dante and I decided to walk one of the trails through the forest out of view from everyone. When no one was looking we ran full speed through the forest. We stopped when we made it to the village of saga toriimoto in Kyoto. It only took us a little over an hour to get here running. We scoped the village before following a trail out the forest. It truly is a beautiful village. Too bad we're not here for vacation. Arobi's dojo is in the back of Arashiyama's bamboo grows. It has several gardens, living quarters, tea houses, and a tall gate protecting it from intruders. We looked at each other and took a deep breath. Arashi and I looked at Dante. It was time for us to split up. Arashi and I will take the hidden trails we know and

Dante will take the one's he and Rin knows. Dante nodded at us and disappeared into the forest.

"Ready." I asked Arashi.

"As ready as I can get. Let's kick some ass." Arashi said smiling.

We disappeared back into the forest, swinging and leaping off trees. We were giggling and laughing all the way, letting them know we were here. We finally leaped over the gate and landed in the back of the dojo where Arashi and I use to train. It's quiet. No one is in sight. Arashi and I scoped out the place and found nothing. No one was here.

"That's weird." Arashi said.

"Something is up. I can feel it." I said looking at Arashi.

"Where's Dante? He should have been here by now." Arashi said.

"Thank you for returning my son to me. I was starting to wander what happen to him." Rin said from inside the dojo. Arashi and I both snapped our attention to where the voice came from. Finally Rin stepped out with a low smile on his face.

"I doubt that Rin. You never been the father type." I said with the same low smile on my face.

"Adena that's not a nice thing to say. That almost hurt my feelings." Rin said grabbing his chest.

"To bad. I will just have to try harder." I snapped back.

"You're almost likeable Adena. Maybe I'll keep you around for my amusement." Rin said laughing.

"Cut the bullshit Rin. Where's Quentin?" Arashi snapped at Rin.

"Arashi. I heard you like a good fight." Rin said smiling at Arashi.

"Then give me one." Arashi snapped.

"Always the eager one I see. Be careful what you ask for Arashi." Rin said dropping his smile.

"Always am." Arashi said.

"Where is Quentin and Dante Rin?" I asked again since he didn't answer Arashi question.

"You will see them soon. First I have some entertainment for you. Think of it as a welcome back present." Rin grinned. "I want them alive." Rin said to his men.

"Good luck with that." Arashi said.

They surrounded us. Rin men were coming from all sides. Arashi and I was stuck in the middle back to back. We moved in a circular motion analyzing our surroundings. More men were coming from over the gate and swinging from the trees. Rin was prepared but not prepared enough if he thought a bunch of ninja's could stop us.

"Let's play." I said to Arashi. Arashi smiled back at me and gave me an acknowledging nod.

Arashi leaped attacking everyone in the air as I moved full speed attacking everyone on the ground. I disarmed two of Rin men of their swords, using them to decapitate them. With one swift move back to the middle I decapitated every men in sight. I looked up and saw more men jumping the gate and leaped up spinning with blades extended out slicing through, causing them to drop to their deaths. Arashi and I landed back to back in the middle where we started. I still had the two swords I took off Rin men and Arashi was holding a polearm with an axe at the end of it. We moved in sequence taking turns taking Rin men out from top and bottom. We cut off men legs and heads with little effort. We blocked their flying knives and attempts to catch us with nets. It was clear that Rin was just using them as a distraction because when I glanced back up at the dojo, Rin was gone.

"ENOUGH!" I yelled. My eyes filled with red and dissipated every one of Rin's men.

"Um Adena. When did you start doing that?" Arashi asked since I never did it before.

"Since now." I said looking at Arashi.

"Lose the red eyes before you dissipate me as well." Arashi said waving her hand at me.

"Arashi you know I wouldn't." I said laughing bringing my normal eyes back.

"When did you learn that?" Arashi asked.

"Nathaniel taught me how to tap into that side of me without using my anger." I explained.

"Is that all he taught you?" Arashi said teasing.

"Really Arashi. Right now is not the time." I said glaring at her.

"It might be the only time depending on what else Rin have up his sleeve." Arashi said focusing her attention back on the dojo.

We knew Rin was in the dojo somewhere. He wouldn't have lured us here just to run away. We decided to split up. I know, never a good idea but it was the only way to cover more ground. Arashi went to look for Dante, while I looked for Quentin. We split.

I noticed Rin had made changes to Arobi's dojo. There were more halls. No lights or windows to let light in from outside. It almost felt like a maze. I looked between the halls deciding which one I was going to take first and saw a shadow moving down the hall on my right. I ran full speed down the hall trying to catch the shadow but it was moving just as fast as I was. I was taken back.

Was it Arashi or Dante? But why will they run from me. I kept going in and out of the halls taking the leading turns with no other options for shortcuts. I saw a light ahead and rushed to it and was suddenly short stop by a hard kick to my chest cracking my chest bone and sending me flying to hit the floor hard back in the dark hall. I staggered to get back up and blacked out falling back to the floor.

I was awaken by a voice in my head. *"Adena get up. Get up now. We don't have that much time. Adena. Adena open your eyes."*

I opened my eyes and tried to get up but my legs were broke. I started to look around and my eyes fell on Arashi and Dante. They both were here, legs broke, tied up and Arashi gagged. I looked at Dante furious. "Who the hell was that that attacked us? You didn't tell us Rin was teaming up with someone like us." I snapped at Dante.

"I didn't know Adena. I never seen him before." Dante explained.

I didn't want to wait for any more surprises so I quickly healed myself and went to break Dante chains as Arashi healed herself and broke out of her chains. "Arashi what happened? Why didn't you free yourself and Dante?" I said confused by her allowing them to capture her, tie, and gag her up.

"Because they had you Adena. I had to make sure you were ok. When I couldn't connect with you mentally I gave in and let them take me. I guess that's something else we didn't know about each other. We don't have our mental connection when one of us is unconscious. I had to wait for you to come back." Arashi explained pissed that Rin knew something about us that we didn't.

"Who attacked us Arashi? Did you see him? Do we know him?" I asked Arashi looking around for the best way out. When I finally looked back at Arashi her head was down and she looked sad. "Arashi what is it? What's wrong?" I asked confused. When Arashi opened her mouth to answer me a door opened. We all got ready to fight our way out but I froze at the sight of Quentin. When I registered it was really Quentin, I ran to him and threw myself around him, kissing him and hugging him tight. I felt Quentin tense and turned around to see Arashi and Dante crouched down ready to attack.

"Get away from him." Dante snapped.

"Dante what are you doing? This is Quentin. Arashi what's wrong?" I asked them both confused. I placed myself in front of Quentin blocking him from Arashi and Dante.

"He's the one who attacked us." Dante snapped.

"That's impossible." I snapped back.

"Adena it's true." Arashi said not taking her eyes off Quentin.

"Arashi I would have known. It's not possible." I said confused.

"Adena remember when we first meet Nathaniel and Joel. We couldn't really sense them either. We only sensed what they wanted us to sense. Quentin been keeping who he really is from you all this time." Arashi explained.

She was right about Nathaniel and Joel. I'm lost for words so I turned and faced Quentin. Looking into his eyes, I was waiting for him to tell me it wasn't true. It couldn't be. Quentin lifted his hand and rubbed his fingers across my cheek with a pained look on his face. I put my hand on top of his and looked up at him holding his gaze. He pulled his hand from under mine and dropped it to his side and let go letting me sense him. I almost choked off how dominant his presence was. My eyes shot wide open. It was true. Quentin is like us but he felt stronger. I stepped back away from him shaking my head no. I didn't want to believe it.

"Adena." Quentin said reaching out to me.

Before I knew it Dante had ran past me attacking Quentin with Arashi not too far behind him. I watched as Quentin blocked, twist away and dodge all their attempts. It felt unreal. I watched Quentin move like he was dancing to a ballet never taking his eyes off me. I wanted to move. Move away from his view but he held my gaze preventing me from moving. Suddenly Quentin gave both Arashi and Dante a blow to their stomachs sending them flying back to where I was standing.

"Adena please. It's not what you think." Quentin said raising his hand in the air as a gesture to surrender.

"How long Quentin? How long have you known?" I asked pissed.

"About me. All my life. About you. When we first met." Quentin said making my mouth drop open more.

"Why didn't you tell me?" I asked.

"I don't know. I wanted to but I didn't want to mess up what we have. I love you Adena." Quentin said making me more furious.

"Enough to attack me and side with a man wanting to kill us." I snapped back.

"It's not what you think Adena." Quentin said.

"Then explain it to me Quentin." I snapped back.

"I will. Just not now. I came to get you out of here." Quentin said.

"After you put us in here." Dante snapped.

"I had to. I'm sorry." Quentin replied giving Dante a warning glance.

"Where's Rin?" I asked.

"You will see him soon. I need you to trust me." Quentin said extending his hand out to me.

I was hurt. Too hurt to even move. Trust him. What the hell makes him think I would trust him after this? I'm furious. The only thing I want to do is rip his head off right now.

"We can take him Adena. Just give me the ok. We haven't been using our full strength." Arashi said using our mental connection.

"And neither has he Arashi. He's been holding back. Even just now when you and Dante attacked him. He never took his eyes off me. I don't trust him right now but it's the only way were

going to get out of here and see what Rin really wants from us."
I said not taking my eyes off Quentin.

I walked over to Quentin and took his hand.

"What the hell are you doing Adena?" Dante snapped at me.

"I know you don't trust Quentin but trust me." I said looking back at Dante.

"I'm not sure that's a good idea right now." Dante said looking back and forth from me to Quentin.

"Well don't trust me, trust Arashi. Either way we're leaving." I snapped back at Dante.

Dante looked to Arashi and Arashi nodded her head in agreement to Dante. They both looked at me. I nodded to them and looked up at Quentin. Quentin squeezed my hand and turned to walk out the door. We followed Quentin in silence. Looking around the dojo. Rin made a lot of changes to the dojo but kept some of its original structure. I don't know where we are going but we walked pass Arobi's room. It looked as if it never been touched. I looked back at it as we walked past it and felt Quentin squeeze my hand. I looked up at him and he gazed down at me with a look of understanding, almost like he knew how much Arobi meant to me.

I wanted to ask him how did he know but I didn't. I dropped my eyes and continued walking. The rest of the walk was very intense. I felt Arashi and Dante walking behind us ready to attack at any given moment. I tried to stay relax but neither of us actually relaxed until we saw light coming from the end of the hall. We prepared ourselves for the worst and was ready for whatever we were walking into. Quentin was either leading us into another trap or he was really trying to help us get out.

Chapter Fourteen

We entered a large room. To our left was the exit to the back of the dojo where Arashi and I came in at. Rin was in the room training. He finished off the men he was training with and turned to face us.

"Aw what a lovely reunion." Rin said giving us one of his cocky smiles. Neither one of us responded to him. We just watched him waiting to see what game he was playing.

"Quentin have you forgotten already what side you're on?" Rin asked Quentin noticing we were holding hands.

"I did everything you asked me to do Rin. Now let them go." Quentin snapped.

"Not everything Quentin." Rin snapped back.

"I won't" Quentin said.

"Let's ask Adena what she thinks." Rin said and turned his gaze to me.

"Quentin what's going on? What else does he want you do? What aren't you telling me?" I snapped and let go of Quentin hand.

"Yes Quentin what else do I want you to do?" Rin added.

"To kill you." Quentin finally said holding my gaze.

I immediately turned my gaze to glare at Rin. "What do you have on him to think that he will kill me?" I asked.

"If you must know. He has the choice to kill you and save his mother or save you and kill his mother." Rin stated.

"Fine." I snapped at Rin. I'm tired of people using me as an option to kill or save someone. Especially when the option always ends with me being the one who has to die.

"WHAT! Adena what are you doing?" Arashi snapped.

"You can't be serious?" Dante snapped.

"I won't." Quentin snapped.

I kept my eyes on Rin ignoring all the protest behind

me. "If Quentin kills me you give him his mother back. If I defeat him you give me his mother and I'll gladly kill you." I said to Rin.

"No I will kill him." Dante added.

"Ok. Dante will kill you." I restated.

"Why would I agree to something that doesn't benefit me at all? Quentin would purposely lose the fight." Rin said.

"True. Well I'll make it hard for him to throw the fight. If he wins you give him his mother back. If he loses you kill her." I said turning my gaze to Quentin. Quentin mouth dropped open and he froze in spot.

"Adena why are you doing this?" Quentin asked pissed that I would even put him in the position to choose.

"Why are you? You knew what he wanted and helped him this far. You might as well finish what you started to save your mother." I snapped at Quentin.

"I won't." Quentin snapped back at me.

"Then die and shortly after that your mother will join you." I snapped intent ally trying to piss Quentin off.

"Um Adena I don't think this is a good idea." Arashi said noticing how angry Quentin was getting.

"Arashi I need you to trust me on this. Please." I said to Arashi not taking my eyes off Quentin. He was really angry.

I didn't wait for Quentin to calm himself down. I attacked. I jumped up kicking Quentin in the chest with both feet and flipped back landing six feet away from him on my feet. My kick did nothing to Quentin. He didn't move an inch nor did it look like he was really affected by it. I tapped into my other strength without getting angry and attacked Quentin again. This time he fought back, twisting, turning, and blocking all my attempts to hit him. In the mist of me throwing a punch he grabbed my fist and squeezed it, making my nails go through my palm. I took the pain and threw a high kick. Quentin blocked it and gave me a blow to my stomach that sent me flying back across the room. I flipped back landing on my feet but slid a few more inches back from the impact of the blow. Quentin didn't wait for me to come at him this time. In a blink of an eye he was suddenly right in front of me. He swung and I dodged his hit by flipping back on my hands and kicking my legs up hitting him under his chin. Quentin fell back. The kick was enough to only infuriate him more.

He rushed me giving me hit after hit. I blocked and twisted my way out of them but Quentin was moving faster than I thought was possible. I blocked another kick twisting around to avoid it and when I made it back around to face Quentin, he grabbed my neck pushing me into the wall. He tightened his grip as I tried kicking and punching him so he can loosen his grip but his grip only got stronger.

I couldn't breathe. I'm losing consciousness. Suddenly Quentin was grabbed from behind and thrown away from me. I felt Arashi come to my side checking to see if I was ok.

"Joel, Rin." Arashi called out.

I opened my eyes to get a glance of Joel catching Rin when he tried to run, surprised by Nathaniel and Joel sudden presence. Dante helped restrain Rin while Quentin and Nathaniel fought.

"Adena…..Adena….are you ok? Adena look at me." Arashi said trying to get my attention.

I focused my attention back to Quentin and Nathaniel.

They both were very powerful and Nathaniel was really going after Quentin. Quentin came at Nathaniel with what it looked like everything he had but Nathaniel was too strong. Nathaniel grabbed Quentin and slammed him to the ground. Quentin tried to get up but was forced back down by Nathaniel foot on his neck. Nathaniel pressed down harder on Quentin neck intending to kill him. I tried to scream stop but nothing came out so I pushed past Arashi and ran to them. I fell next to Quentin and looked up at Nathaniel.

"Nathaniel please stop. Don't kill him. Please." I pleaded with Nathaniel. He was so far gone. His eyes hard already turned grey. I didn't know how to convince him to stop so I got on my feet and walked up to him. I stood next to him and turned his face to get his gaze on me. When I had his gaze I brought my face to his and kissed him. I wrapped my arms around his neck and put every ounce of breath I had in me to kiss him. I felt Nathaniel lift his foot off Quentin neck. He picked me up and wrapped my legs around his waist. I let him take control since I was too weak to hold on. I tried to keep up with his intense kiss but I could no longer breathe. I pulled back and gasped for air.

"Adena." Nathaniel said sitting us down on the ground.

"Adena are you ok? What were you thinking? That could not have happened how you intended it to. I could have hurt you." Nathaniel snapped at me.

"I….I…..I…knew….you….wouldn't." I said gasping for air.

"Shhh. Don't talk. Catch your breath." Nathaniel said.

"Then….. Stop……asking …..Me …..Questions." I gasped again.

"Stop talking Adena." Nathaniel snapped and rolled his eyes at me.

I took a couple of deep breaths and got up. I walked over to Quentin to check on him.

"Is there a reason why you stopped me from killing him when he was trying to kill you?" Nathaniel snapped at me.

"This is Quentin." I said looking up at Nathaniel from Quentin side. Nathaniel froze. I saw all the anger come back to him that instant.

"Nathaniel don't. Please. It's not what you think. Rin has his mother. He was going to kill her if Quentin didn't kill me. Quentin didn't want to but I forced his hand." I blurted out real fast trying to get Nathaniel to back down. "Nathaniel Please." I pleaded again. Nathaniel relaxed and looked at me holding my gaze. I broke the connection and looked back down at Quentin.

"Adena I don't accept that. He's strong enough to have beaten it out of him and you could have got that information out of Rin too." Nathaniel Snapped.

"What.....what do you mean?" I asked Nathaniel.

"Remember what you told me happened when you tried to kill Seth. How you read his thoughts just by touching him." Nathaniel explained.

"I wasn't myself when I did that. I don't know how I did it." I said putting my head down ashamed I didn't think of that.

"WHAT!" Quentin snapped. "You put me through all of this and could have read Rins mind." Quentin got up and towered over me.

"Quentin I'm sorry. I didn't realize." I said putting my head down again.

"You have nothing to apologize for Adena. You don't know how you did it before." Arashi said coming to my side and pulling me up off the ground.

"I should have tried." I said.

"Adena you are not responsible for this." Arashi said trying to stop me from blaming myself.

"You proud of yourself Quentin. She tries to help you and you blame her." Arashi snapped at Quentin.

"Tried to help me by getting me to kill her." Quentin snapped back.

"And almost succeeded if it wasn't for Nathaniel." Arashi snapped again.

"Stop fighting. It's not helping either of us solve anything. Where's Rin?" I snapped turning my gaze to where Joel and Dante stood with Rin between them.

"What are you doing Adena?" Nathaniel asked.

"I'm about to try to read Rin mind." I said walking over to Rin.

"Adena I thought we had a deal." Rin said with his same cocky smile on his face.

"Rin. Shut up." I said placing my hands on his head. I tried to concentrate on what he was thinking but nothing happen.

"Nothing. I got nothing." I said.

"Try again. This time tap into your anger and focus." Nathaniel said coming behind me. I tried again this time tapping into my anger. I focused but nothing happened.

"Nothing." I said again.

"Adena try getting a little angrier because you were beyond angry that day." Arashi said.

I looked back at her and tapped completely into my anger making my eyes turn pitch red. I turned my gaze back on Rin and squeezed his head harder. I focused but was about to lose my control. I tapped a little more into my anger and heard Rin scream out from the pressure of me squeezing his head. All his thoughts came crashing into me. There were so many thoughts and memories. Evil, sad, happy, anxious, and to my surprise love. I finally seen where he held Quentin mother and let go of his head. I concentrated on letting go of my anger and felt my eyes change back. I looked back at Quentin.

"He is holding your mother in Arobi's room. She's in a hidden safe in the floor." I stated. Quentin gave me an acknowledging nod and disappeared down one of the halls. We all turned our gaze back to Rin.

"What was the point of all this Rin?" Arashi asked.

"He wanted to kill the one thing he thought his father loved better than him." I answered.

Bruce walked up to Rin and gave him the scroll Arobi hide with information about who we were.

"What are you doing Bruce? We need that scroll." I snapped surprised by what Bruce just did.

"It's okay Adena. I read the scroll. Arobi left it for Rin." Bruce said.

"I don't understand. I thought it was about who we are or where we came from at least." I said.

"It's about you in some ways. It explains to Rin why you are so important to Arobi. It's a personal message to his son." Bruce said urging Rin to open it.

Dante untied Rin and allowed him to read the scroll. We all watched for his reaction to see what Arobi said. Rin looked up at Bruce and Bruce nodded in agreement to whatever Arobi put in the scroll for Rin. Rin looked around to all of us and looked back at Bruce and nodded back in agreement.

"What the hell does that mean? What was all this bullshit for?" I asked pissed that all our lives were interrupted for an agreeing nod between family.

"Adena calm down." Bruce said.

"I will not. He did everything he could to kill us. Even use my boyfriend who turned out to be one of us to kill me. My life has been turned upside down and all the answer I get is an acknowledging nod between you two. I'm sorry Bruce but that is bullshit. We all came here for information about who we really are and this is it." I snapped pissed off about everything. I almost died today and it was for nothing.

"I'm sorry for what I did Adena. I didn't realize what my father was doing. I understand now and I promise to keep what I know about you all a secret. There will be no more attempts to kill you from me." Rin stated. I walked up to Rin and stopped in front of him. I looked at him for a long minute then punch him. I was so mad the punch sent him flying into the wall.

Quentin came up and put his hand on my shoulder
and I grabbed and twisted his arm, then sent him
flying across the room. I turned to face everybody and
they all moved back.

"Adena you have to calm down." Nathaniel said not
moving from the spot he is standing in. I just looked at
him and held his gaze. Everything around me was red.
I couldn't calm down, I was getting angrier and angrier
the longer I stood there. I wanted to go. Get away
from them. Suddenly I blinked out and was now in the
hotel room.

I felt myself breathing hard and concentrated on
slowing my breathing. I calmed down and my vision
came back to normal. I still didn't want to be here so I
packed my stuff and left. I didn't want to sit in the
airport waiting on an available flight back home so I
ran. I stopped only to drink water from lakes and
oceans on the way. I ran wanting to forget everything.
Wanting to get away from everything.

Chapter Fifteen

I ran for hours, days, maybe even a week. I wasn't
sure. I just wanted to get away. Wanted to go home
but I couldn't because I knew that Arashi would be
there waiting for me. I didn't feel like talking about
what happened. I didn't want to confront or be
confronted by Quentin. I didn't want to see Arashi and
Joel happily ever after. I didn't want to hear Bruce
explanation of that damn scroll.

I just wanted to be away from everybody, go
somewhere I was safe, and go somewhere I didn't
have to talk. I kept running, running to nowhere,
hungry, dehydrated, tired, and still pissed. I ran and ran
wanting to be somewhere safe. Needing to be
somewhere safe and suddenly I blinked out of the
forest I was running through and was suddenly in

someone's place. It looked familiar but what was I doing here? Why did I come here?

I heard footsteps coming down the hall. I crouched down getting ready to attack. I waited and waited for whoever was going to come down the hall. Finally they came and I froze. Froze not able to move. He froze me in spot with his gaze.

"Adena." Nathaniel said.

I looked around the place again and realized now why it was so familiar. I'm in Nathaniel's place. Why? Why am I here? I heard Nathaniel call my name again and snapped my vision back to him. He walked towards me with his hands in the air. I took a step back keeping my eyes on him. Why was I here? I still can't answer my own question.

"Adena can I get you something? Are you hungry?" Nathaniel asked. Obviously he noticed my raged look. I looked like a wild animal who escaped from the wild. I realized then how hungry I am. It's been days since I've eaten. Yes I was hungry. Yes. But something else was taking me over. I was losing consciousness. I tried to pull myself together. Focus on Nathaniel coming towards me but I couldn't. I couldn't hold on anymore. I let the darkness take me over. I was gone.

"Adena come on baby. Open your eyes for me. Adena!" Nathaniel said shaking me.

I tried to do what he said and open my eyes but something is hitting me in my face. It's cold and wet. I finally got my eyes open. It's water. Nathaniel was holding me under the water in the shower. I fought against him wanting to get out. Wanting to get away but he held me there. Wouldn't let me go.

"Stop fighting me Adena." Nathaniel snapped.

"Let me go. Let me go now!" I snapped.

Nathaniel let me go. I pushed past him and ran out the shower. I still had my clothes on and they were drenched from the shower. I was still weak. I collapsed to my knees coughing. What the hell was wrong with me? I finally stop coughing and just laid down on the floor. I didn't have the strength to move anymore so I just laid there. Laid there and went to sleep.

I woke up in a large bedroom. I knew I had to be in Nathaniel's room. I was in a t-shirt. I looked around the room for my clothes and didn't find them. My underwear was also gone. I heard Nathaniel footsteps and climbed back in the bed and got under the blanket to hide myself. It was pointless since I know he was the one to undress me and put me in this t-shirt. He was taking care of me and I'm being weird because I don't know why I brought myself here. I wanted to go somewhere safe. Somewhere where I wouldn't be bothered.

Nathaniel entered the room with a tray of food in his hands. My stomach started to growl and I realized I still haven't eaten. The pulling in my stomach is so painful. I looked at Nathaniel and he just watched me. Watched me for what felt like forever.

Nathaniel finally started walking towards me slowly. He made it to the bed and set the tray at the end of the bed. He looked at me and walked away. He walked over to the window where there was a lazy boy couch. He sat down and didn't say a word. I watched him for a minute before my stomach pulled again urging me to eat. I couldn't put it off any longer. I pulled the tray to me and started to eat. I was too hungry to care about Nathaniel seeing me eat like a savage. I couldn't stop. I licked the plate clean and wished I had more. I was still hungry but the food was enough to shortly satisfy me. Nathaniel rose from his chair and walked towards me. I froze not knowing what he was going to do. He didn't speak to me. Didn't ask me anything. I don't know why but I was grateful. I didn't want to talk about anything. He simply reached for the tray, took it and walked out of the room.

I relaxed for a minute until my stomach growled again. I knew I was still hungry but I thought I would be okay for now. I heard Nathaniel footsteps again. What could it be now? He was standing in the doorway with the same tray again. He repeated the same steps as the first time.

He walked slowly to me and placed the tray at the end of the bed. He looked at me and then walked back over to sit in his chair. I watched him. He always seem to know what I wanted. He knew I was still hungry without me saying it. I looked at him for another long minute and then grabbed the tray. This time I took my time eating.

I noticed that he made me breakfast. Pancake, eggs,

hash browns, and sausages. This time he gave me a full glass of apple juice. I didn't have one the first time. I looked at him in appreciation and this time picked up my utensils to eat. I cut my pancakes up and poured syrup on them. Also something I didn't have at first. He knew I was going to attack my plate the first time. I ate in silence once again. When I finished this time I was full. Nathaniel got up again and got the tray and left the room. Hopefully he doesn't bring me anymore food but I knew he wouldn't. He seemed to know me so well. I realized I knew exactly why I came here to Nathaniel. I do feel safe with him. I knew he would know exactly what I wanted. What I needed.

I just sat here on the bed not knowing what to do with myself. I kind of stink. I needed a shower but wasn't sure if I should get up and take a shower. Before I could answer my own question, Nathaniel was back. He was holding two towels in his hand. He didn't say anything. He just walked over to the bed and held his hand out to me. He watched me trying to see what I will do. I sat there for a minute and then leaped out the bed and took his hand.

He led me to the bathroom still holding my hand. When we made it into the bathroom he let go of my hand to throw the towels over the shower and turn the water on. After he was done he walked up to me and reached down to grab the hem of the t-shirt he put on me. I lifted my arms straight up so he can pull the shirt over my head. He stepped back, paused a minute not taking his eyes off me and started to take his clothes off. He had on a white tank top and some red pajama pants that hanged from his waist.

I took a deep breath but said nothing. I waited for him without protest. He walked over to the shower and pulled the door back. He held out his hand for me and I took it with no hesitation this time. I climbed in and he followed right behind me. The shower was big enough for us to fit comfortably. It was big enough to hold a few more people in it.

This time I walked into the water and relaxed as soon as the hot water hit my skin. It felt so good against my skin and I lost myself in it. Nathaniel came up behind me and turned me around. He held my gaze before holding his hands up. He was holding a shower sponge in one hand and body wash in the other. I took my gaze back to him and nodded my approval.

I put my head back under the water as he washed my body. I felt his hands grip my waist and brought my head back up to look at him. He turned me around and started washing my back. Feeling his hands slowly going down my back and working in a circular motions down.

It felt so good that I had to put my face under the water to try to keep myself from moaning. When he was done washing my body, he began to wash my hair. I didn't protest. I just pushed my head back into his massaging fingers. I felt like purring like a cat to his touch. When he was done I was kind of angry because it felt so good and he took the feeling away.

When he turned me around to lean my head back so he can wash the shampoo out, my anger must have been showing on my face because when he was finished he washed my hair again. I purred like a cat this time letting it out. I didn't care about him hearing me. It felt too good.

This time when he was finished I just looked up at him

holding his gaze. He grabbed my waist again and moved me behind him. He stepped into the water and washed himself. I stood there watching him like a predator. I couldn't take my eyes off him. Off his body. I counted every visible muscle I could see. I wanted to rub my hands across every one of them to see if they felt as smooth and hard as they looked. Time seem to have flown by because I felt like it was over too fast. I wanted to watch him some more. Wanted to stay but Nathaniel turned the water off and lead me out the shower. He dried us both off and wrapped towels around us.

It was the same routine for the next few days. Nathaniel fed me, washed me, and spent time with me. We watched television, listen to music, and went for walks. He treated me like I was his girlfriend but without the conversation. It felt good. I was happy. He didn't ask me any questions. Not even if I was okay. He knew I was. He made sure I was. I often looked at him to see if he was getting tired of taking care of me. If he was ready for me to leave, or if I was irritating him with my silence but he looked happy.

He looked like he was okay with me being here. I wanted to say something but I didn't want to ruin this for either of us. I knew he was waiting on me to say something but I felt as if he also needed the silence so I said nothing. At the end of the day we went to bed. He always held me tight against him and kept me pulled into him all night. Every morning I woke up in his arms and felt safe. I don't know why I needed to feel safe, but I did.

I watched him as he slept this morning. He looked so relaxed and peaceful. When he finally woke up, he caught my gaze. He held my gaze looking deep into my eyes trying to figure out what I was thinking. He finally took his fingers and rubbed them down my cheek. I finally decided to speak.

"Good morning." I said.

"Good morning baby." He said making me blush. For some reason I liked when he called me baby. I looked back up at him and he was smiling at me. Noticing my reaction to him calling me baby. I didn't speak again. I just waited. Waited to see how he wanted today to go.

"How do you feel?" Nathaniel finally asked.

"I feel good. Really good. Thank you." I said truthfully.

"Good." Nathaniel said then smiled.

After spending so many days not talking I wanted to talk to him. I wanted to spend more time with him but I knew this had to come to an end soon. I looked down at my hands twisting them around trying to hide my thoughts from him. I know he can read me like a book and I still wasn't ready to face anything.

To go back to a life I don't feel comfortable about anymore. I just wanted to be normal. Whatever that meant. Just for a little while longer. Nathaniel put his hand under my chin lifting my face back up to him. I look into his eyes as he searched mines and did my best to hide everything I was just feeling. He shifted up on his elbow and looked down at me.

"Come on. Let's get some breakfast." Nathaniel said.

"Okay." I said glad we weren't about to have some awkward conversation with each other.

We got up and headed to the kitchen. As usual he held my hand leading the way. It felt good not to have to be in control all the time. Felt good to let him take care of everything while I follow his lead.

We made it to the kitchen and started moving around each other like an old married couple. He pulled out everything he needed to make breakfast as I put water in the teapot and put it on the back burners to boil so Nathaniel could use the front ones to quickly make breakfast. I pulled out a tea mug for me and a glass for Nathaniel. Poured Nathaniel some orange juice to go with his breakfast and then grabbed the plates and utensils for us to eat with. We moved in sequence around each other. We were always close to each other but never in each other's way.

I heard the teapot squeaking when it was ready and went to get my tea bag and sugar cubes. I sat down and waited for Nathaniel to pour the steaming water in my cup so I can prepare my tea. I knew better to reach over the stove to get the tea pot and I just knew he was going to get it for me. After he poured my water and put the tea pot back on the stove he made our plates.

While he did that, I reached for some napkins and placed one on each side of our plates. Nathaniel went back in the refrigerator and grabbed some apple juice for me. He knew I wasn't going to drink my tea until it cooled down a little bit and that I always wanted apple juice with my breakfast. I smiled and waited for him to sit down before I ate.

We finished our food and Nathaniel took our plates and placed them in the sink. He held his hand out for me and I took it. He led me to the bathroom where we washed our faces and brushed our teeth. I noticed that I had my own toothbrush and towel set. I don't know why I didn't notice it before but it was nice. When we were done Nathaniel led us back to the front room and turned on the news so he can catch up on current events. I went back into the kitchen to clean the dishes.

"You don't have to do that Adena." Nathaniel said walking towards the kitchen.

"It's okay. I don't mind. Besides it's the least I can do." I said smiling back at him.

"You keep that up I might not let you leave." Nathaniel said teasing.

"How do you know you not already stuck with me?" I

teased back.

"You better stop that before you end up in my kitchen barefoot and pregnant." He said coming behind me pulling me into him.

I laughed and hit him in the side with my elbow. "Go away." I said waving my hand for him to get out the kitchen.

"As you wish." He whispered in my ear making me shiver. The connection we have is good. I was lost in it and then his phone rang. I was so far gone I didn't even realize how disconnected we were from reality.

I finished washing the dishes and joined Nathaniel in the living room. I don't know who he's talking to but he kept his eyes on me. He gave the person on the phone short answers and his face started to frown up. I was curious to know who was messing up his mood but stayed silent and sat next to him. He pulled me into him and laid my head on his chest as I tried to watch the current events on the news. Really didn't interest me so I kept my eyes on the television and listen to the rest of Nathaniel conversation.

"I told you fine. Stop asking me." He snapped at

whoever was on the other line.

"Yea.......and.......I won't. Not until." He paused for a minute and then continued. "Just no." He finally said. There was a short pause and then Nathaniel snapped.

"I'M SELFISH!" Nathaniel snapped at his phone. "YOU HAVEN'T SEEN ME BE SELFISH YET!" He snapped again. "TRY IT AND I'LL FUCKING KILL YOU!" He snapped before slamming his phone down.

I didn't know what to do so I just sat there, not moving, pretending to watch the news. I felt him calm down and run his hands through my hair.

"I know you're not watching television Adena. You hate the news." Nathaniel said in a calm tone.

I laughed. "You're right. I do hate the news. I just didn't want to be nosey." I said.

"I'm sorry about that." Nathaniel said pulling my face up to look at him.

"It's okay." I said and smiled. I watched his face frown up like he wanted to tell me something but like me, he didn't want to kill the connection we have. I knew it was time to face the world again just by the expression on his face.

"What's wrong Nathaniel? Who was that?" I asked trying to keep a straight face without looking disappointed.

"We can talk about it later. What do you want to do today?" He asked trying to change the direction the conversation was going in.

I just stared at him. Searching his face for something. Something to tell me what that was all about but Nathaniel was good at hiding things. I waited and waited for something. I wasn't sure what but nothing was there. He looked at me and smiled. Smiled because he knew I was lost. He knew I couldn't read him like he read me. It was irritating. He leaned down and placed a kiss on my forehead then went to get up. "Come on. Let's go for a walk." He said.

"I......I don't have anything to wear." I said looking down at the t-shirt I still had on. When we went walking the other times I wore his jogging pants and t-shirts. I didn't care how I looked because I was still adjusting. Now that I'm back I want to wear my own clothes. Feel like a girl again. I looked back up at him and he was smiling.

"Of course you do." He said.

"I don't want to wear your clothes. I want to wear mine Nathaniel." I said giving him a sour look. He just held his hand out to me. I waited for a minute looking at his hand and then finally got up and walked to him. He led me back to his room and into his closet. We walked into his walk-in closet and I put my head down not wanting to wear his clothes. I appreciated him letting me wear his clothes but I really wanted to wear my clothes today.

He stopped in front of a rack in the middle of the closet and squeezed my hand. I took a deep breath and looked up at him a little mad. I didn't want to go for a walk anymore. He looked at me and tilted his head urging me to look in front of me so I did.

"My clothes." I said reaching to touch them and feel them. They were really my clothes. I looked at him grinning from ear to ear. "How?" I asked.

"I went to your place and got some of your clothes when......" He stopped not wanting to say anything to upset me.

"It's okay. Thank you so much Nathaniel." I said and reached up and kissed him on the cheek. His face lit up. That was the first time I really seen him smile. He looked undeniable. It made me blush.

"You welcome. I'll leave you to get dress." Nathaniel said and walked out the closet.

We took a long walk around downtown Chicago. I love Michigan Avenue. It was beautiful out today. It felt good to feel the breeze against my skin. Nathaniel made our time out today really special. He took me out for lunch, took me shopping, and treated me like I was the only girl in the world. I was his girl today. If it was a real date he definitely would have got some tonight. The thought made me laugh.

It was such a good day I didn't want it to end. I knew whatever we had to talk about was something we both wanted to avoid. I knew he made today special because it was the last day we will spend together like this. It made me sad but I knew I had to accept it.

When we made it back to Nathaniel place we both were a little sad. We gripped each other hands and took a deep breath.

"How was today?" Nathaniel asked.

"It was great. Thank you for all of this." I said referencing to everything.

"Anytime." He said smiling. We sat in silence for a few more minutes holding on to what we were about to give up.

"Are you going to tell me what that phone conversation was about?" I finally asked Nathaniel.

He took a deep breath. "It was Joel. He was calling to check on you." Nathaniel said putting his head down.

"It had to be more than that Nathaniel. Especially for you to threaten to kill him." I said.

"They accused me of being selfish for keeping you here and not letting them come to see you. Joel said he was going to come and take you away from me. Take you home with them." Nathaniel said with his face tensing up with anger just by thinking about it.

"I see." I said.

"I'm sorry if I made you feel like a hostage here." Nathaniel said.

My mouth dropped. I instantly got pissed. "Nathaniel

you made me feel worshiped. You gave me everything I wanted. You made me feel safe. I didn't want to have to deal with anything, or talk to anyone. I just wanted to be exactly where I was. I came to you. I'm pissed they would make you feel that way and I'm going to give them a piece of my mind." I snapped.

"I will love to see that baby but I understand. I didn't want to share you." He admitted.

"I didn't want you to either." I admitted.

"What do you want to do Adena?" Nathaniel asked.

"Stay sucked up in our little bubble we created." I said.

"I have no problem with that." Nathaniel said smiling.

I laughed and watched as we got sucked in our bubble again. I knew it was wrong. I knew Arashi was worried and I was also being selfish hiding from her and letting Nathaniel keep them away. It was time for me to face everyone and go back to whatever life had waiting for me now.

"I guess it's time to face everyone." I stated a little sad.

"If you want to wait Adena you can. Just tell me and I'll kick whoever ass that try to come through that door." Nathaniel said holding my gaze.

"Thank you Nathaniel. But I think it's time I face the firing squad." I said.

"The hell it is. I'll kill them all." He snapped.

I laughed and hugged him. I love how protective he is. It gave me the strength to suck it up and go back to reality.

"Do you want them to come here?" Nathaniel asked.

"No. Can we go to them? I don't want them to mess up our vibe here just in case I need to run back." I said.

"Of course and you can come back anytime you want. Promise me you'll come back if you need to." Nathaniel said holding my gaze once again.

"I will." I said. We ended the night the same as the rest. I cuddled up in his arms. I made sure I snugged tight in his arms and drifted off to sleep.

Chapter Sixteen

It's morning. I knew it because I felt the sun shining in on us. I felt the heat of its presence on me. I didn't open my eyes because I needed a few more minutes to adjust before going back into my old routine. I took a deep breath and waited.

"It's okay if you still need time baby." I heard Nathaniel say.

I opened my eyes and faced him. "I'm okay. I rather get it over with." I said and then smiled at Nathaniel.

"Ok. Breakfast?" He asked.

"Yes please." I answered.

He got out of bed and held his hand out for me. I got up and reached for his hand. He pulled me into him and held me close to him. He looked down at me holding my gaze and I waited to see what he would do. My body was yearning for him but I didn't move. If he wanted to have me right now he could but he just held me close to him. So close I felt every ab muscle on his stomach and the rise of his cock the longer he held me there. He just searched my eyes for my response but he knew it already.

He knew he could have me but he didn't. He pulled back, grabbed my hand and led me to the kitchen. We went back into routine. Eat, shower, brush our teeth, and this time get dressed. We went back in the front room and watched a little television. My favorite show was on. I loved charmed. They always played the reruns in the morning. Nathaniel didn't bother me while I watched my show. He just held me and kept me warm up against him. In the mist of the show his phone ranged.

"WHAT!" He shouted. I knew then it had to be Joel again. Who knew he would ever be so nasty with Joel. He always been so protective of him but I guess things changed.

"We'll come to you when we're ready." He said. "Get

off my ass Joel. If she wants to stay she can fucking stay. I don't give a fuck about what you'll want. She said she want to come today so we'll come when she's ready." Nathaniel snapped. There was another pause. I looked up to see if he was still on the phone. He was. He held my gaze and rubbed his hand down my cheek. "Look Joel we'll be there. Stop busting my balls. It's too damn early for this shit." Nathaniel said calming down a bit.

I smiled at him and laid back on his chest. Charmed was about to go off. I liked supernatural but I didn't need to watch it like I needed to watch charmed. Nathaniel got off the phone as charmed went off and I shifted off him just in case he needed to get up. He pulled me back into him.

"We can stay as long as you like. It's early. You don't have to deal with their shit this early." He said.

"Okay." I said and pressed my head back into his chest. "You can turn if you want. I know my shows are kind of weird." I said.

"It's okay baby. I don't mind. I can watch you while you watch TV." He said.

I lifted my head up to smile at him and then continued watching my show. Supernatural came on three times before actually going off. I looked up at Nathaniel to see what he wanted to do now and he was already staring at me. I smiled and shook my head.

"Where are they? I mean where are we going?" I asked wandering if they were at Arashi's house or at the safe house.

"Arashi's house." He answered.

"Joel and Arashi have gotten pretty close." I stated.

"Yea. They're supposedly in love." Nathaniel said rolling his eyes.

I Laughed. "Let me guess you don't approve." I said.

"I'm happy for them. They're just irritating together and Joel's confidence has made his head big. I'm surprised I haven't kicked his ass yet." Nathaniel said shaking his head.

"He broke out of his shell. I'm sure Arashi made sure of that." I smiled up at Nathaniel.

"I guess. Are you ready to face the lovebirds?" Nathaniel asked.

"As ready as I'm going to get." I smiled and got up.

Nathaniel pulled me back down. This time to straddle over his lap. I took in a breath and held it. I looked at his intense expression and waited. Waited to see what he was going to do next. He grabbed my waist and lifted me up with him as he got up off the couch. "Ready." He said and put me down. He grabbed his keys and we finally left. Left our bubble not sure how things were going to be after today between us.

Chapter Seventeen

We arrived at Arashi's house. He pulled up in front of the house and turned the car off. We just sat there looking at each other for a long minute.

"We can still leave if you want to." Nathaniel said.

"The hell you will!" Arashi snapped standing in front of the car.

"I have no problem running you over Arashi." Nathaniel said.

"Over my dead body." Joel said joining Arashi at the front of the car.

Nathaniel rolled his eyes at both of them and looked at me. "Just say the word baby." He said. I smiled and caressed his cheek.

"It's okay Nathaniel. Thank you." I said.

I got out the car. Before I could close the car door Arashi was on me. She hugged me so tight I couldn't breathe. She finally pulled back and starred at me. Looked me up and down and then gave a sour look back at Nathaniel. I couldn't help but smile. I guess it was too soon because Arashi snapped her attention back at me and went off.

"Don't you ever do that again to me Adena! I was worried out of my mind. Not sure if you were okay, not sure if you needed me, and I couldn't feel you. We had no connection at all. What the hell were you thinking?" Arashi snapped. I didn't know where to start.

"Can you scream at me in the house? I would like some tea before you cut my head off." I said.

Arashi didn't say anything. She hugged me again and then ushered everyone into the house. The tension between her, Joel, and Nathaniel weighed heavy in the air. It was almost unbearable to see. I couldn't take it no more.

"I don't understand why you'll being so hostile towards Nathaniel. If it wasn't for him I wouldn't be here now. If you don't want him here then I will leave with him." I stated with a bit of anger in my tone.

"He kept you away from us Adena. He wouldn't let us come over, he wouldn't let us speak to you, and he wouldn't even update us on how you were doing. He didn't even answer our phone calls majority of the time. We popped up over there and he went hell raiser on us. Didn't lets us in." Arashi snapped not taking her eyes off Nathaniel.

"And I'll do it again." Nathaniel snapped back.

"It's okay Nathaniel." I said not wanting him to take the blame for what I wanted. "Arashi I couldn't. I didn't want to see anybody. I didn't want anybody to see me. I just wanted to be alone. Wanted to get away. I didn't even talk to Nathaniel and he managed to give me everything I needed and wanted without any input from me. He willed me back." I said turning my gaze to Nathaniel and smiling at him.

"But…." Arashi started to say.

"I'm sorry for putting you through that but don't take it out on Nathaniel. He was just doing what I wanted. Giving me what I needed. Something only he could have done. I know that sounds mean but it's the truth." I said watching Arashi reaction.

"Adena we would have all taken care of you and did whatever you needed us to do." Arashi said.

"I know Arashi but you wouldn't have been able to do it without me telling you what I needed. At the time I didn't even know what that was. Nathaniel always known how to read me. He always known exactly what I needed and wanted. He was really there for me the way I needed him to be. He was only looking out for me. He knew I wasn't ready to face any of you yet." I said walking up to Arashi to get her attention. To bring her gaze to me and off of Nathaniel. "You have to trust me Arashi. You know Nathaniel wouldn't have been that hard on Joel for nothing." I stated trying to open her eyes to see it from my point of view.

"I get it Adena but I'm still pissed." Arashi said.

"Okay. Just take it out on me not Nathaniel." I said.

"Are you going to tell us what happened?" Joel said jumping to the point.

"Leave her alone Joel she just walked in the door." Nathaniel snapped.

"I was just asking Nathaniel. I'm sure she doesn't need a bodyguard." Joel snapped back.

"This is so weird. Can you two stop? I will answer all your question after I get some tea and sit down." I snapped.

Nathaniel and Joel looked at each other and made their way to the living room while Arashi and I went to the kitchen. Arashi knew how I liked my tea. She made my tea for me and slid it in front of me.

"You want a muffin? I have some blueberry one's here." Arashi asked.

"My favorite. Thank you." I smiled because Arashi never did anything for me when I was here. She always told me to get it myself. That I'm not a guest.

"Are you really ok Adena? The last time I saw you, you were off the walls mad." Arashi asked.

"I'm fine now. Much better. Calmer I think." I said with a low smile.

"Quentin been by a couple of times to check on you. I just told him you were ok and we'll know more later." Arashi said. She stared at me waiting for my reaction. I knew it was going to come up soon.

"Thanks." Was all I could say. I wasn't ready to deal with Quentin yet. Not yet.

"You and Nathaniel seem to be closer. Are you two together now?" Arashi asked.

"We are closer. We're not together. He's just being protective of me Arashi." I said knowing this was going somewhere. Not just where.

"It's just I don't think you should run to Nathaniel just because things went wrong with Quentin. Quentin really loves you and he kept his secret for the same reason you kept ours from him. He didn't want to hurt you Adena." Arashi scrambled out the words fast so that I wouldn't interrupt her.

"Arashi, me going to Nathaniel had nothing to do with me running from Quentin. Yes I'm pissed at Quentin but this was about me not him." I said.

"Are you going to talk to him?" Arashi asked.

"Eventually. Not today. I need more time." I said to Arashi.

"Oh." Arashi said. I just knew she did something by the look on her face and the sudden change in her voice.

"I know that look Arashi. What did you do?" I demanded.

"I kind of told Quentin you were coming over today." Arashi said.

"WHAT! HOW COULD YOU ARASHI? THAT WAS NOT YOUR PLACE!" I snapped. If it was her goal to piss me off. She succeeded.

"You need to face him Adena. Besides all this was to get him back. Now that he's back you won't even talk to him." Arashi said defending herself.

"This is isn't about him Arashi. It's about me. It's my decision to decide when I want to talk to him not yours. I knew I shouldn't have come here." I snapped aware that my last statement would hurt her.

Arashi mouth dropped open. I saw the rage rise in her face. We stood there just staring at each other. Neither one of us giving in. I kept my eyes on Arashi.

"Nathaniel." I screamed his name.

Nathaniel and Joel ran to the kitchen to see what was wrong. Arashi and I were still staring at each other not giving in. Nathaniel and Joel were side by side looking around to see if someone else was there. They focused back on me and Arashi intense stare at each other.

"What happened?" Nathaniel snapped.

"We're leaving." I snapped back.

Nathaniel walked over to me and put his hand under my chin. He lifted my head so I can look at him but I kept my gaze on Arashi. I wouldn't take my eyes off her. Nathaniel walked in front of me and blocked my view of Arashi.

"Baby what happened? What's going on?" Nathaniel asked in a calmer tone.

"Does it matter?" I snapped again.

"No." He said a little pissed by my tone. "If you want to go we can go." Nathaniel finally said holding my gaze.

"Arashi what happened?" Joel demanded. When Arashi didn't answer him, Joel pulled Arashi into him and demanded an answer from her.

"Arashi I won't ask again." Joel snapped.

"I told her that I told Quentin she was coming today." Arashi finally snapped at him.

"WHAT!" Joel and Nathaniel snapped together.

"Why the hell will you do that Arashi?" Nathaniel

snapped.

"What's the matter scared she'll run to Quentin this time." Arashi snapped at Nathaniel.

It took everything Nathaniel had to control his anger. His presence got stronger and we all knew he was pissed.

"Arashi that was out of line." Joel snapped.

"She need to talk to him Joel. Us going there was for him and she's avoiding him." Arashi said to Joel.

"Today was not the day Arashi." Joel snapped.

"Maybe not but who knew how long Nathaniel was going to keep her away from us this time." Arashi said turning her gaze back at Nathaniel.

"FOREVER!" Nathaniel snapped and grabbed my hand and headed out the door.

"Adena you know I'm right." Arashi said as we went out the door. I looked back at her and just shook my head. I couldn't believe she would do that. We use to be so connected. She should have known that I didn't want to see him. That I needed more time.

Nathaniel opened my car door and I got in. He strapped me in and I just sat there and let him do whatever he needed to. He hurried to the driver's side, got in and pulled off. He was still fuming. We were speeding on the expressway. Weaving in and out of traffic. I didn't want to disturb him. I knew he would calm down eventually. When we were almost back at his house he had calmed down. I guess sitting at the red light gave him time to breathe his way through his anger. The light turned green and he looked over at me. It felt like a long minute had passed before he finally pulled off. I reached over and placed my hand in his. I pulled his hand to my mouth and kissed his knuckles. I felt him relax.

We finally made it back to his place. When we walked in to his place we both relaxed a little more. Our hands still entwined with each other. Nathaniel pulled me into him and I slammed into his chest.

I looked up into his eyes searching for what he was about to do. He leaned down and kissed me. Really kissed me. Before I knew it he slipped his tongue in my mouth and pushed his mouth deeper into mine. He wrapped his tongue around mine owning it with his own. I threw my arms around his neck and kissed him

back. The intensity of the kiss had me boiling over.
I wanted him and wanted him to take me. I tried
pulling his head into me some more. Stepping on my
toes and giving myself completely to him in that kiss.
Nathaniel picked me up and wrapped my legs around
his waist. I tightened my hold around him as he walked
us into his bedroom. He laid me on the bed and
hovered over me. He pulled up and stared down at
me.

He watched as I breathe hard waiting for him. I didn't
want him to stop so I moved my vagina up and down
him over and over his dick. I felt his dick rise and push
against the fabric of his pants. He let out a low moan
and I tilted my head back in appreciation. Nathaniel
leaned down and kissed me on my neck. He was gentle
at first sending vibrations down my body. Then he
started to suck. Suck hard on my neck and I felt it
down below. I tilted up into him and reached for his
shirt. I pulled at his shirt wanting him to take off. He
grabbed the back of his shirt and pulled it over his
head. I took my hands all over him. I moaned at the
smoothness of his skin. I wanted him. Wanted him

now.

Nathaniel started to undress me. He slowly pulled my shirt over my head and tossed it off the side of the bed. He rubbed his hand down the middle of my chest until he reached my bra. He rubbed his hand across each of my breast making me push up into his hands. When he made it back to the center, he yanked my bra off, breaking the straps, and tearing the latch. It was a complete turn on. I gasped and arched my back into the air as it caressed my nipples with its cool presence. Nathaniel watched me as I struggled to control myself under him.

He used his feet to kick my shoes off while he unbuckled my pants and pulled them, along with my panties off at the same time. I was completely naked under him. He got up and stood staring down at me. I laid there with my hands to my side to control myself. I wanted him so bad and the more he stood there just staring at me, the wetter I got. I couldn't take it any more so I lifted my hand out to him urging him to come get me.

He looked at my hand and then back into my gaze.

Without taking his eyes off mine, he kicked off his shoes and pulled his pants and briefs down. His dick sprang out and up. My heart felt like it skipped a beat. He was so hard and so big. I couldn't take my eyes off him.

I watched as Nathaniel came back over me using his legs to separate mine. I spread my legs with no hesitation then wrapped them back around his waist. He gripped my thighs and then pushed them apart making them spread up and out until they touched the bed. I was wide open and felt every ounce of air hit my clitoris.

I moaned and grabbed my breast. I looked at Nathaniel and started to play with my breast. Teasing him by teasing myself. I squeezed and pinched my nipples until they were sensitive and hard. I watched Nathaniel reaction.

He licked his lips and admired the view. I knew he wasn't going to last any longer. He looked as if the beast in him was ready to explode. He leaned down and took one of my nipples into his mouth. The heat from his mouth alone almost made me explode. I tried to lift up into him but I couldn't move.

His grip on my thighs was unbreakable. I felt his hands press in more into my thighs and lifted them up some more. My knees were almost next to the sides of my breast. I moaned and moaned and waited. Waited for him to take me. I needed him in me now. Right now. Nathaniel looked down at me. He did nothing until I looked at him. He held my gaze. Held me there watching me. Finally he lowered his self and let his dick rub against the lips of my pussy. He pressed down a little more and his dick spread my pussy lips and pressed hard against my clit.

I groaned loud and hard. Without skipping a beat, I felt Nathaniel move his hips back and slowly, finally, but very slowly slid into me. I started shaking all over. He froze after he pushed the head in and waited for my shaking to calm down. I tried arching up into him to take all of him in me but his grip was still too tight. I couldn't move a muscle.

 I gave up trying and waited on him. When he saw I stop trying to push up against him and my shaking had calmed he continued. He continued his slow torture. I felt every inch of him as he slowly slide in me. I gripped the sheets in my fist as he pushed further into me. I felt full but he wasn't done. He kept pushing into me slowly. My mouth opened and my eyes closed tight.

"AH! Nathaniel. AH!!!" I screamed. I felt so many things at once. He felt so good inside me. I felt pleasure and pain. I wanted more but felt like I couldn't take anymore. I moaned harder arching my back. I finally felt his skin touch mine. He arched more into me pushing me up on the bed. I let out a small scream taking him. Taking all of him.

"AH! SHIT!" Nathaniel said and looked down at me. "Open your eyes Adena." He demanded. I did as I was told and looked into his eyes. They were grey. I knew he was barely holding on. He was going to cum. He was going to cum soon. He pulled back and I felt every inch of his dick as he pulled out of me. He stopped with the head still in me.

"Ready?" He asked.

"Yes." I said letting out a breath.

Nathaniel plunged into me. I screamed from the

intensity of the pain and then moaned from the pleasure it gave me. He plunged into me again. Over and over. Faster and Faster and I exploded. I screamed my orgasm out. I heard Nathaniel scream his out as he came with me. It was hypnotic and hard but Nathaniel was still going.

I felt him cum but he was still hard. Still plugging into me. I felt another orgasm rising in me. I tried to control it but I couldn't. I came again. Exploding all over again. I felt my eyes roll back. I felt myself go limp as Nathaniel released his second one. He plunged one last time into me and then collapsed on top of me. I was to gone to feel the pressure of his body weight. We just laid there. Laid there waiting for the sensation to stop running through us. We both were still shaky a little. Nathaniel finally pulled out of me and made me gasp from the sensitivity of my clitoris. He fell on the side of me and pulled me into his embrace. He held me tighter than he have ever had before. It felt good. I snuggled into him and went to sleep.

Chapter Eighteen

I woke up and stretched out. My thighs hurt a little but I feel great. I noticed its dark outside. I must have slept a long time. Nathaniel wasn't in the bed. I wondered where he went. I sat up and leaned against the headboard for a minute.

 I remembered that Nathaniel threw his t-shirt on the side of the bed and went to get it. I found it and put it on. I got out the bed and stood there listening for Nathaniel footsteps. I didn't hear anything so I headed to the bathroom. I really had to pee. It was so quiet in here and I didn't want Nathaniel to hear me pee. Weird I know but

I felt weird about peeing in front of him. I made it to the bathroom and went straight to it. I sat down and relaxed. Pee started flowing out of me and it felt so good. I felt like I was holding it forever. I let out a deep breath, wiped myself, washed my hands and headed back to the bedroom. There was still no Nathaniel. I stood there with my arms folded a little pissed that he was gone.

"Hey baby." Nathaniel said from behind me.

I jumped. He scared the shit out of me. "Hey." I said after catching my breath.

He laughed. "Sorry didn't mean to scare you." Nathaniel said with a huge grin on his face.

"It's okay." I said.

"Were you looking for me?" Nathaniel asked walking up to me and stopping right in front of me making me look up at him.

"Yes." I said.

"I'm here." He said wrapping his arms around me.

"It was extra quiet in here. I thought you left." I admitted.

"No. I was outside on the balcony looking over the city. Are you okay? Do you need something?" Nathaniel asked pushing me back to look over me.

"I'm fine." I stated.

"Did I hurt you?" He asked. I knew he was talking about during sex.

"Yes. But I liked it." I admitted shyly.

"Sorry. I couldn't hold back anymore. I had to have you." Nathaniel said pulling me into him.

"And I you." I responded. I laid my head on his chest and wrapped my arms around him. He ran his fingers through my hair and we stood like this for the next few minutes.

Nathaniel picked me up and wrapped my legs around his waist again.

"Ouch." I winced from the pain.

"That bad huh?" Nathaniel asked.

"It's ok. I can take it." I said wrapping my arms around his neck and actually managing a teasing smile.

"I'm tempted to test that theory Adena. You better not tease me." Nathaniel said laying me back on the bed. He hovered over me pressing me down into the bed with his weight. He looked at me holding my gaze. I looked into his and smiled. I don't know what he's thinking but I was happy being right where I was. He finally laid on the side of me and pulled me into him.

"Go back to sleep baby." He said.

"But I can't sleep. Can't we do something to change that?" I asked pushing my butt back into his dick to give him a hint.

"No. Go to sleep." Nathaniel said smacking me on the ass. I laughed and wiggled my butt against him some more.

"Unless you want me to fuck your ass Adena, you better not get me railed up again." Nathaniel said kissing my neck. I froze. I heard Nathaniel laugh.

"I knew that would stop you." He said.

I pouted and just laid there in Nathaniel arms. I wasn't sleepy anymore. I feel like I have all the energy in the world right now. I felt Nathaniel arms go heavy over me. I knew he was fast asleep. What can I do? I don't want to sleep. I want more of him. I turned around to face him. I threw my leg around him and used my body weight to push him on his back. I waited to see if I had woken him but I didn't. He had on his pajama pants and they had an elastic waist. I smiled knowing exactly what I was going to do.

I eased myself between his legs and hovered over him. I watched his breathing for any indication that he was about to wake up. He was out. In a deep sleep. I smiled harder and reached into his pajama pants and grabbed his dick.

He moaned and lifted his hips pushing his dick further into my hand. I held tight onto his dick and watched to see if he was waking up. Nothing. It was now or never so I leaned down and took him in my mouth. I took my tongue slowly around his head and worked my way down the rest of his dick. I sucked moving up and down his dick in a slow motion.

Nathaniel moaned again and pushed his dick further into my mouth. I took him in gratefully. I used my hand to squeeze his dick harder as I sucked and rolled my tongue around his head. I took him deeper in my mouth and sucked like he was my very own lollipop. I felt Nathaniel hands go in my hair and grip my head. I sucked harder and faster increasing my up and down motion.

"AH! SHIT! ADENA!" I heard Nathaniel call out. I ignored him and finished my assault on his dick. I started moving my hand up and down at the same rhythm as my mouth.

"HOLY FUCK!" Nathaniel screamed out. I felt his hands grip tighter in my hair. I felt him raise his head and knew he was looking down at me. I kept my eyes closed not wanting to break my rhythm.

"ADENA! SHIT! I'm about to cum baby." Nathaniel said. I moaned and kept going. I knew he was about to come in my mouth but I didn't care. Not right now. I had to keep going. I fought through the pain in my cheeks and kept going. I felt his dick harden in my mouth making it almost impossible to hold him in. He was so thick and long but I managed to keep him in my mouth.

"ADENA!" I heard Nathaniel say and he let go. I kept pumping his dick with my hand taking in all his cum. I swallowed and swallowed until I swallowed every last drop. I kept a hard grip on his dick as I pulled it out my mouth and licked the head one last time. I felt the shiver that went through his body. I released my hold on his dick and hovered over him. Nathaniel pulled me into him and held me tight against him.

"Damn Adena." Nathaniel said rubbing his hands up and down my back.

"I told you I wasn't sleepy yet." I said happy with myself.

"I hear you loud and clear now baby. Loud and clear." Nathaniel said.

I smiled against his chest and knew he felt me grinning from ear to ear. We laid there a few more minutes. Nathaniel pulled me up to look at me. I looked back and forth between his eyes then leaned down and rubbed my nose against his. Next thing I knew, Nathaniel had flipped us over and he was now on top of me. I gasped in surprise of the sudden turn in events.

"My turn." Nathaniel said and went down. Before I had time to take a deep breath he was opening my pussy lips with his tongue. He didn't hesitate. His tongue dived right into my pussy and went to work. He lick, pushed into my walls and sucked over and over. I couldn't keep still. I was moving and pushing up against him. Nathaniel grabbed my thighs and pulled me into him keeping me still. I couldn't move.

Couldn't wiggle to control the sensation. He made me take it all. Made me feel it all. Nathaniel moved on to my clit. He gave it one hard lick and I wanted to combust.

"NATHANIEL." I screamed. I put my hands in his hair and pulled. I pulled his hair but it did nothing. He could not be moved. He took my clit into his mouth and sucked. He sucked hard and then harder. He sucked one more time and then used his tongue and gave my clit one hard ass lick and I exploded.

"AH!!!" I screamed and screamed, shaking uncontrollably. Nathaniel didn't stop. He kept licking and sucking on my clit. He brought me sensation after sensation. I was building up again. I was at the edge. I couldn't hold on. I exploded again. It was too much. Too much. I couldn't take no more but Nathaniel kept going. He worked me up again.

"Nathaniel please." I begged.

"Please…..AH…..PLEASE!" I screamed and then came again. I fell limp. I was so overwhelmed. Over satisfied.

I felt Nathaniel fingers caress my side and I couldn't

take it. The feeling was overwhelming. I smacked his hands off me and started shaking my head no. I couldn't take no more.

"Nathaniel please." I pleaded with him.

"Are you sleepy now?" Nathaniel asked.

"Yes." I said barely comprehending what he said. I was lost. Lost in wonderland somewhere.

"To bad. I'm not." He said. I didn't know what that meant until he slammed into me. My eyes shot open. Nathaniel slammed into me over and over.

"NATHANIEL!" I screamed. "AH!" I said from pain this time. He was really giving it to me. All of him. I felt his pelvis hit mine each time he slammed into me. He arched up and his dick started hitting my clitoris each time he slammed into me. He did it one last time and I exploded. Exploded loud and hard.

"AH BABY." Nathaniel said and came shortly after I did. That was it. That's all it took and I was out. Out cold.

Chapter Nineteen

I woke up even more sore then before. I needed to get up and stretch and cursed from the pain caused by my abrupt movement. I looked over at Nathaniel who was sleeping in peace with a satisfied smile on his face. I didn't want to wake him so I took a deep breath and moved slowly off the bed ignoring my pain. When I started to walk to the bathroom I definitely had the just got fucked hard walk. As painful as it was I smiled because the pleasure that got me there was so worth it. I finished up in the bathroom and took my just fucked stroll back to Nathaniel's room. I walked back into the bedroom and noticed Nathaniel was laid out on his back with his hands behind his head, and legs crossed with this huge smile on his face. I knew he wanted to laugh at the way I was walking.

"Love the just fucked walk." Nathaniel said still grinning from ear to ear.

"Abuse in all fifty states you know." I said feeling like I just took a beating. Although pleasurable, my thighs protested the after affects.

"I had to make sure the job was done right. The first round clearly wasn't enough for you." Nathaniel said as he got out of bed and strolled over to me. He bent down and examined my inner thighs and pressed his finger on the folds of my pussy. I winced at his touch and closed my eyes.

"Bath time." Nathaniel said and picked me up so I wouldn't have to walk. When we made it back to the bathroom he put the seat down on the toilet and set me down. He started the bathwater and poured some lavender bubble bath in.

"How did you know I love the scent of lavender?" I asked curious of him knowing exactly what I liked.

"You have lavender everything at your place. When I went to get some of your things I noticed it." Nathaniel said taking a seat on the tub as we waited for it to fill.

I smiled. "Yes. I love the scent of lavender. It calms me." I said and then stretched to test my joints. They still hurt.

"Um stretching won't make that pain go away baby." Nathaniel smiled at me clearly happy with himself.

"Are you going to join me in the tub?" I asked still wanting his company.

"In pain and still want some more. Do you want me to join you Adena?" Nathaniel asked. I knew he just wanted to hear me say it. Wanted to hear me tell him I wanted him.

"I didn't notice you were this cocky before." I said shaking my head at him.

He turned and checked the water. It filled quickly in the huge tub. He turned the water off and walked over to me. He helped me stand up and removed the t-shirt I had on. "That's not an answer Adena." He pointed out.

"Yes but not for sex. I just enjoy your company." I warned and stated.

"Okay." Nathaniel said lifting me and seating me in the tub. I watched him push his pajama pants off and get in the tub behind me. When he was settled he pulled me into him.

"Thank you for taking care of me." I said again so he knew I really appreciated it.

"Thank you for trusting me enough to come to me. You looked like you were lost, starving, and dehydrated when you popped up here." He stated massaging my shoulders.

"I was. I was tired and wanted to go home but knew I couldn't. I knew Arashi would be wherever I went and I just didn't feel like facing anybody. I was hurt. Still hurt. I just wanted to feel safe. I ran and ran thinking over and over in my head that I just want to be safe. Safe from everybody. Safe and quiet." I said closing my eyes and remembering the feeling I had when I was running. Running away from everyone. I felt betrayed, used, helpless, and weak. Four feelings I never faced before and never wished to again.

"Is that why you came here?" Nathaniel asked as he used his fingertips to softly caress down my arms.

"At the time I didn't know why I came here. I was running and thinking about being safe, then all of a sudden I was here in your place. It wasn't until I saw you that I figured out where I was. It didn't sink in why until after I realized you were taking care of me." I said running my hands up down his legs as we talked. "Why?" Nathaniel asked.

I thought about it for a minute before I answered. I knew the answer but I wasn't sure if I wanted to admit to it yet. I took a deep breath and said "you make me feel safe Nathaniel. I didn't want to admit that to myself. I would still be denying it if my conscious didn't bring me here. I was still denying it even after I saw you. Before I blacked out I kept asking myself why did I come here." I told him.

"There's something between us Adena. We can't ignore it anymore." Nathaniel stated as he turned my face to look up at him. I turned to face him wrapping my legs around him.

"I know." I said holding his gaze.

He was right. In the short time we known each other, our attraction and need for each other was stronger than the one I felt with Quentin. I thought Quentin was the one for me. That he was it. Even ignored my feelings for Nathaniel to convince myself that Quentin was it for me. Now I was confused. I still love Quentin but I think I love Nathaniel too.

I lowered my gaze from Nathaniel's. I didn't want him to see my confusion about Quentin.

"You're thinking about him. Quentin." Nathaniel stated.

"I......I.....don't understand why. We barely know each other but it feels like I've known you forever. I thought Quentin was it for me but now I'm confused. With everything that happened, what he kept from me, I'm pissed at him. I still love him but I'm broken now. I don't see him the same way. I know I need to talk to him but my body and heart is running in the opposite direction. I don't know if I'm running to you or if I'm supposed to be with you. I just can't explain this pull I have to be with you." I said shaking my head from confusion.

"We'll figure it out together." Nathaniel said taking his fingers across my cheek.

"What if I hurt you?" I asked

"You won't" Nathaniel smiled.

"Why are you so sure?" I frowned at him.

"I just know what I feel Adena. I'm confident about that." Nathaniel said.

"Maybe you should have enough confidence for the both of us." I said trying to manage a small smile.

"I got you baby." Nathaniel said smiling and pulling me into his embrace.

I smiled and wrapped my arms around his neck. I loved hearing him call me baby. It felt good. I felt like I was a normal girl spending time with my normal boyfriend.

We relaxed in the tub for a little bit longer before finally getting out and starting our unknown day.

"I need to talk to Arashi. Hey do you know where my phone is?" I asked feeling weird without it now.

"Yes I have it. I turned it off when you first came so it wouldn't disturb you." Nathaniel said waiting for my reaction.

"I understand. Can I have it now?" I asked.

"Of course." Nathaniel said as he walked to a drawer in the kitchen and pulled it out. He brought it over to me and set next to me on the couch.

"Thank you." I said turning my phone on hoping it was charged.

"You welcome. I kept it charged for you." Nathaniel said watching his daily intake of the news.

"Oh. Thanks." I said again.

"Adena you don't have to keep thanking me. I'm happy to do whatever you need from me." Nathaniel said giving me a stern look. I smiled and returned my focus back on my phone.

"WOW!" I shouted. "I have a lot of missed calls and messages." I said going through them.

"Yea. They been trying to reach you every day since you split." Nathaniel said flicking threw the channels looking for something else to watch. He settled on The Godfather.

"This was very irresponsible of me. I should have at least eased everyone mind. Plus we still have a business to run. I left everything to fall on Arashi. My clients can't be happy about not being able to get in touch with me." I said angry that I completely fell of the face of the earth.

"You needed time Adena. Don't beat yourself up."

313

Nathaniel tried comforting me but I was still pissed. I was too wrapped up in our bubble. "Adena don't." Nathaniel snapped as if he can read my mind.

"I need to call Arashi." I said as I dialed her number.

"Hello." Arashi answered.

"Hey are you busy." I asked.

"No what's up." She asked unsure of my mood.

"I want to get together. Just me and you to talk." I said.

"Okay. I'm free." Arashi said.

"How about around 3 at the Grand Lux Café?" I loved that restaurant and I know Arashi like it as well.

"Okay. See you then." Arashi said and the call ended.

"So you ditching me?" Nathaniel said with a playful smile on his face.

"To the curb." I said smiling and making a hand gesture pointing to an invisible curb.

"Ouch!" Nathaniel said moving his hand to his chest in a playful gesture.

"Move it Ike." I said smiling and getting up to get some juice from his fridge.

Nathaniel grabbed me and pulled me into his lap.

"Ana May don't temp me." He said right before
tickling me. I bust out into a loud laugh trying to get
away from him. He pinned me down under him on the
couch and tickled me relentlessly.

"Nathaniel stop." I cried out. I was laughing too hard
and couldn't take no more. Nathaniel tickled me a little
more before he finally stopped. When he let me up I
didn't hesitate. I lunged at him full speed tackling him
but Nathaniel was fast. He caught me twisting us and
landed on top of me with a primal smile on his face.

"Hmmm was that an attempt to turn me on or you
really don't like being tickled?" Nathaniel asked
hovering over me.

I smiled then used my legs to push Nathaniel's leg
open into a split causing him to fall into me. I use the
opportunity to flip us and crouch over him. I smiled
down at Nathaniel enjoying the physical activity since I
haven't had a good fight in a while.

"I can think of better ways to turn you on. I love to
laugh Nathaniel so I have no problems with tickling. I
just wanted to test your reflexes." I said still smiling
down at Nathaniel.

"Test my reflexes huh." Nathaniel said using my own move on me, spreading my legs to make me fall into him. He caught me bringing me down to hoover right over him. We were so close the tip of our noses were touching. "How's that baby?" Nathaniel smiled and rubbed his nose to mine.

"Not fare using my own move on me." I said trying to get up but Nathaniel held me close to him.

"It's a very effective move. Why not use it?" Nathaniel said with lust in his eyes. I could see where this was going and I would never make it to meet Arashi on time.

"O no you don't. I have to meet Arashi and I don't want to be late because of my thoroughly fucked walk." I said breaking out of Nathaniel's hold and standing up.

"That a give her something to think about." Nathaniel said smiling while thinking about the expression on Arashi face when she figured out why I was walking that way.

"Men." I said rolling my eyes. "I have to go." I said going for my phone and checking the time.

"I can drive you." Nathaniel offered.

"Thank you but you're literally down the street. I can walk." I said happy to be getting out on my own.

I looked at Nathaniel when he didn't respond. He was still lying on the floor with an intense look on his face. I knew what he was thinking because it was also on my mind. I took a deep breath and went to lay down next to him on the floor.

"So this is it." Nathaniel said.

"Not it. I'm just going to meet Arashi. Get some things straightened out." I said trying to ease his mind. Nathaniel turned on his side, leaning his head on his propped up hand.

"So you're coming back after you leave Arashi?" Nathaniel asked.

I turned and looked at him. "You want me to come back?" I asked holding his gaze.

"I don't want you to leave." Nathaniel admitted frowning.

"I don't want to go." I replied.

"Come back." He said and rubbed his fingers down my cheek.

"Okay." I said shivering from his touch.

Nathaniel held my gaze for another minute before getting up and reaching for my hand. I took his hand getting up and felt weird about the occurred moment we are having. Do we hug, kiss, or pretend like this is just a normal day for us.

"Take the keys." Nathaniel said and kissed me on my cheek.

"I don't know how long I'll be gone. What if you need them?" I asked.

"I'll be fine. Just take them." He said.

I nodded and then smiled heading for the door.

Chapter Twenty

I made it to The Grand Lux Café a few minutes before 3. I knew it wouldn't be crowed at this time so there was no need to get here early for a table. I walked to the desk to request a table for two. I stopped when I saw Arashi already there requesting one.

"Wow! I didn't expect you to be on time." I teased.

"I'm turning over a new leaf." Arashi said as she turned around to face me.

"I like it. Does Joel have something to do with the change?" I asked teasing again.

"Maybe." Arashi smiled at the mention of Joel name. I rolled my eyes and threw my hands in the air as if surrendering to their new found love.

"Your table is ready. Follow me please." The waitress said to us and gestured for us to follow her.

We followed the waitress up the long escalator to the second floor. We were seated in a booth near the window. Arashi and I loved the view of downtown so the table was perfect. We sat down, gave the waitress our drink orders and looked over the menu before placing our order. As usual Arashi and I ordered the same thing. Some things will never change. We looked at each other and laughed.

"Arashi I want to apologize to you for not reaching out to you. I knew better and plus we have a business to run and I left it all on you." I stated.

"Adena I don't mind. You needed some time and that's fine with me. It just hurt that you couldn't come to me. I was so worried." Arashi said with a little hurt on her face.

"I know. I'm sorry. I just needed some time to myself. So many things were going through my head and so many feelings. I just wanted to drop off the face of the earth." I admitted.

"I wanted to kill Quentin for not telling you. And for him to use his full strength on you like that. I was pissed." Arashi said.

"Thanks but that was my fought as well. I shouldn't have provoked him like that. I crossed the line." I told Arashi shaking my head at the memory of what happened between me and Quentin.

"You were just trying to help Adena. He knew that but he still went too far. He almost killed you for heaven's sake." Arashi snapped.

"Yea. I need to be careful what I ask for next time." I said giving a small smile.

"Not funny Adena." Arashi snapped.

"So why did you take Quentin side the other day?" I asked because of how things went the last time we were together.

"I was pissed at Nathaniel. Quentin was wrong but at least he would have let me see you." Arashi said.

"I'm sorry. Nathaniel was just being cautious. I didn't speak to him the first few days. I just popped up in his place and fought him when he tried to help me at first. But he really took care of me." I told Arashi grasping her hand over the table to reassure her that I was okay.

"So did you two fuck yet?" Arashi blurted out being as blunt as usual.

"Arashi!" I said surprised that she would blurt it out like that in the restaurant.

"What? It's a simple question Adena." Arashi rolled her eyes.

"That's not important." I snapped.

"It is if you two did it." Arashi said leaning over the table to catch my gaze. She waited on me to answer.

"Yes." I said clearing my throat and drinking some of my wine.

"I knew it! So who's better? Quentin or Nathaniel?" Arashi asked overly excited.

"The food is taking forever." I said looking for the waitress. I knew the food would distract Arashi. Distract us both from the direction this conversation is going.

"Come on Adena. You have to tell me. Which one?" Arashi demanded.

I opened my mouth to say something and the waiter finally came with our food. I smiled at Arashi and shook my head.

"You're going to say Nathaniel aren't you?" Arashi asked me not giving up.

"Arashi it doesn't matter." I said not wanting to compare the two.

"The hell it does. It will help you make a decision. You definitely want to choose the one that rocks your world the most." Arashi stated while slicing up her steak.

"They both rocked my world Arashi." I stated.

"But which one you can't get enough of? Which one really fucks you like you need it?" Arashi asked.

"Arashi I'm not answering that." I waved my hand at Arashi telling her to get over it.

"Maybe you need to fuck Quentin one more time to see if he'll out do Nathaniel." Arashi started rambling on.

I really wanted off this subject. I do not want to think about having to choose between Quentin and Nathaniel. Not right now any ways.

"How's Bruce and Dante?" I finally asked.

"Worried about you. They know how much you wanted to find answers about us. Bruce understands why you're angry. He wishes he knew more or that Arobi would have just told him." Arashi said giving me a sympathy smile.

"I have to go see him. Where is he and Dante?" I asked.

"Dante stayed with Rin to make sure he was really going to honor Arobi's wishes and not come after of us again. Bruce is at the safe house. He said he enjoy being there in the forest." Arashi said.

"Have my clients been reaching out to you? Are they upset?" I asked.

"Yea they been calling a lot. I panicked at first cause you know I don't know anything about that investment crap but Joel handled it for me. He really is smart. It turns me on to watch him work." Arashi smiled.

"Wow. I have to thank him. I'm a little surprised. I forgot Joel and Nathaniel work was a little similar to ours from a good and bad point of view." I laughed at the thought of me and Arashi being the good guys and Nathaniel and Joel being the bad guys.

"I guess so." Arashi said looking at it from my angle.

"Arashi how would you feel about working together with Nathaniel and Joel?" I asked curious.

"It would be a little weird seeing that they work the assassin angle of things. What's your angle?" Arashi asked me.

"They have a lot of high profile clients who trust them. That can really get our foot in some more corporate opportunities." I said.

"I guess so. We can give it a try. Especially since I'll get to spend more time with Joel." Arashi smiled.

"You see enough of each other all ready." I complained.

"That's because we can't keep our hands off each other." Arashi said winking at me.

"Censor alert." I said not wanting the details.

"I'm glad you're better." Arashi said.

"Me too. I might have missed you a little." I said frowning my face.

"You know you did." Arashi responded back. We laughed and finished the rest of our food. The food was great as usual. When we were done we set back in the booth and relaxed to let the food digest a little before we left.

"What's on your agenda today?" Arashi asked me.

"I'm thinking about going to visit Quentin to get it over with. Then I told Nathaniel I would come back to his place." I said as I reached for the bill to pay.

"That's going to be interesting. I can't wait to find out what happens. You have to call me right after you leave Quentin's." Arashi said revealing her love for reality drama.

"I'll see what I can do." I said shaking my head at Arashi.

"He's going to want to sleep with you. You know that right?" Arashi said.

"Arashi I'm not sleeping with Quentin. I'm just going to talk." I stated.

"Did you tell Nathaniel you were going to see Quentin?" Arashi asked.

"No. So don't you tell Joel. I'll tell Nathaniel when I see him later." I said with a little attitude in it so that Arashi know how serious I am.

"I won't." Arashi smiled as we got up to leave. We hugged each other making up for the time we spent apart and left.

I flagged down a cab and headed to Quentin's place.

Chapter Twenty One

I made it to Quentin's place. I looked up at the building he stays in for a moment before getting out the cab. I paid the cab man and headed up to Quentin's place before I changed my mind. I took the stairs up not wanting to wait on the elevator. It doesn't take long, I just didn't want to wait. When I made it to his door I knocked and stepped back not sure what his reaction would be. In that moment the door swung open and Quentin stood there froze in the doorway. I didn't say anything. I just stood there waiting for him to suck it in that it's really me. Quentin took a breath and held his hand out to me. I stood staring at his waiting hand for a moment then stepped forward and put my hand in his.

Quentin walked backwards pulling me into his place. Once I made it through the door, Quentin yanked my hand making me fall into him. He hugged me so hard I couldn't breathe. I couldn't move. I just waited for him to finish.

"Adena I've been worried. How are you?" Quentin asked releasing me finally.

"Not dead." I snapped not really intending to. I thought I was over my anger but I guess not.

"I deserve that." Quentin said frowning.

"Sorry. I didn't come here to argue. Arashi said you been coming by." I said.

"Yes. I wanted to see you. Make sure you were okay. She told me you were at Nathaniel house. I didn't know if she was just telling me that because she was pissed at me so I kept trying hoping I'll run into you. The other morning I stopped by she told me you were coming over but she didn't know what time." Quentin explained.

"I'm sure Arashi was trying to piss you off but she wasn't lying. She never lies." I said confirming what Arashi said.

"Have you been with him this whole time?" Quentin asked. I could hear the irritation in his voice.

"Quentin don't." I said not wanting to have a conversation about Nathaniel with Quentin.

"Don't what? Ask the woman I love if she's been staying with another man." Quentin snapped.

"Someone you love. Really. Who tries to kill someone they're in love with?" I snapped back.

"You didn't give me a choice Adena. You know I wouldn't hurt you. Not intentionally." Quentin said.

"But you did." I snapped. "You almost killed me. What kind of love is that?"

"Adena I'm sorry." Quentin said reaching for me. I stepped back not wanting him to touch me. I can tell he was hurt from me backing away from him. His eyes watched me, assessing what just happened then he frowned.

"So that's it Adena? You with him now?" Quentin snapped at me.

"I don't know." I said honestly.

"Adena I'm not letting you go. We're in this mess because of you and I'm not about to let you blame me and use it as an excuse to leave. You're mine not his. It's not over." Quentin snapped.

"Quentin……..I…….I'll just leave." I said as I turned to leave.

"Adena don't do this. Don't make me chase you." Quentin snapped.

"Are you shitting me? You almost kill me and demand me, no threaten me to stay. I don't give a fuck how strong you are Quentin. You're never touching me again." I snapped and went for the door. Quentin was in front of me instantly.

"Adena wait. Please don't go. I just want us to go back to how we were with each other. I love you too much to let you go. Please don't leave me angry." Quentin pleaded.

I opened my mouth to say something but Quentin stopped me. Before I knew it he was kissing me. He kissed me as a desperate man fighting to save his family. He put so much passion in the kiss I yielded to him and let the feeling run through me. It felt so good and made me remember how great we were together. I wanted him.

"Don't go." Quentin said pulling me back to look at me.

"Quentin I don't want to fight with you. I just need time." I said pulling away.

"Are you going home?" Quentin asked rubbing his fingers down my cheek.

"No. I'm going back to Nathaniel's after I stop home and get some of my things." I said.

Quentin froze. I can feel the tension rising in him again. I never seen this side of Quentin before because we never had a reason to fight before. I watched Quentin gaze go cold and heartless.

"You're not going back to his place Adena." Quentin snapped gripping my arms.

"Yes I am Quentin. Now let me go." I snapped as I pulled myself out his grip.

"I'M NOT GOING TO SIT BACK AND LET YOU FUCK SOMEOTHER GUY!" Quentin snapped making me jump.

"FUCK YOU QUENTIN!" I snapped back rushing to the door. I slammed his door on my way out.

I ran down the stairs and out the double doors of his

building. I couldn't get out of there fast enough. I looked around to see if I could spot a cab. I needed to get away. I just ran. Ran all the way home. Although it wasn't that far, seeing my home calmed me down a little. I took a couple of deep breaths and went in the house. I went straight to my room, kicked off my shoes, and laid back on my bed. I closed my eyes and tried to relax until my phone rung. Irritated by the disturbance I answered.

"WHAT!" I snapped into my phone.

"That's not a good greeting baby. I take it your lunch with Arashi didn't go very well." Nathaniel said cheerfully on the phone.

"Oh. I'm sorry Nathaniel. Everything went fine at lunch. Arashi and I made up." I said in a calm tone.

"Where are you? I was thinking about ordering something for dinner." Nathaniel asked.

"I'm at home. My place. I wanted to get some more stuff." I said.

"How are you getting back here?" Nathaniel asked.

"I might call a cab." I said sounding a little tired.

"I'll come get you." Nathaniel offered.

"You don't have to. What are you ordering for dinner?" I asked.

"I'm thinking Friday's. I'll order, come pick you up, and then we can pick the food up together. You sound tired. Let me come get you Adena." Nathaniel said using his take charge voice.

"Okay. I'll wait for you." I agreed.

"On my way." Nathaniel said and then ended the call. I laid in my bed a few more minutes. I probably had a good fifteen minutes before Nathaniel got here. I got up and packed some more underwear and some of my work out clothes. I grabbed some casual and business clothes just in case I had to meet with my clients. When I was done I looked around my place like it was the last time I would see it. I knew I would be back but it just felt like I was leaving. In the mist of me giving a silent goodbye to my place someone knocked on the door. I looked at my watch and realized time either flew by or Nathaniel drove like a bat out of hell here. I opened the door and saw Nathaniel standing in the door way with a huge smile on his face.

"Hey baby." Nathaniel said making me smile. He

always made me feel better when he called me baby.

"Hi." I responded and opened the door wider to let Nathaniel in. "I just have to grab my bag and I'm ready." I said.

"Take your time." Nathaniel said as I closed the door behind him. I walked to my room and grabbed my bag.

"Okay I'm ready." I said coming back to the front room.

"Moving in baby?" Nathaniel asked noticing how big my bag was.

"No. I just didn't know how long I will be at your place and I need my business clothes just in case I have to meet my clients." I explained.

"You don't have to explain. My place is your place. I got your bag. Let's go." Nathaniel said walking up to me and grabbing my bag. He kissed me on the cheek making me give him a shy smile. Nathaniel opened the door so we can leave and we were blocked in. Blocked in and surprised by the pissed off person at my door. This day couldn't get any worse.

"Quentin."

Coming in March 2015

~ ~

~

Perplexed

~ ~

~ ~

Find out what happened between Adena, Quentin, and Nathaniel in the second installment of the Confound trilogy.

TERESA LUCAS

Meet the Author

Teresa Lucas

Thank you so much for reading Confound. I hope you continue reading and enjoy the rest of the series.